The Ballad of Billy Turner

By Bryan Corbin

The Ballad of Billy Turner

BJ & AK Books
ISBN-13: 978-0615759562 (Custom)
ISBN-10: 0615759564

Book designed by Jim Gullett

*This book is dedicated to my precious son Patrick,
who more than anyone else inspired this story.
I pray that he will one day understand the incredible value of
who God made him to be.*

Acknowledgments

It is impossible to grasp all of the love and support that brought this story about, but all credit must begin with my Lord and Savior – Jesus Christ and pass through the beautiful family that He's raised up around me. Together they are all of the inspiration that I could ever need. I also need to acknowledge two special young men, Jimmy Gullett & David Bonar; whose lives (along with my son Patrick's) helped to form the basis for the character of Billy.

Special thanks to:

My Wife – for so often seeing what I cannot.
My Children – for helping me to view the world through new eyes.
My Mother – for believing that what appeared to be a defect was actually a gift.
My Brothers and Sister – for their unwavering encouragement, support and patience.
My Nana (Eileen Doherty) – for showing me that God wants to be involved in our day to day.
Gary and Pam Kellough - for teaching me about the fruit and the invisible war.
Kevin Elliot and Wayne Campbell - for showing me the door way.
Mark and Nicki Pfeifer - for helping me to see what is unseen.
Don and Barbara Atkin - for showing me a walk of integrity.
Aaron and Rachel Hines – for their humility, transparency and contagious passion for the Lord.
Bruce and Laura Hambrick - for their encouragement and support.
Daryl Wood – for clarifying commas, colons, and capitalization.
The Billy Turner Fan Club (Karla, Vikki & Marilyn) – for being a special part of Billy's upbringing.
Jimmy Gullett – for putting all the pieces together.

Table of Contents

Foreword

When a musician plays an instrument, it isn't really the musician that we hear. It is actually the instrument's response to the promptings of the musician. With the brass and the woodwinds it is the player's breath moving through the inner parts of the instrument, or with the stringed instruments it is the sound of the strings resonating in response to the musician's touch. The unique construction of each instrument conveys the breath and/or touch in a different way, thereby creating a completely distinct sound. And so it is with God and all that He has created. The Father is the Master Craftsman who handcrafts each instrument, winnowing out the inner chambers of every heart and fastening every heartstring. The Spirit is the Master Musician, whose deft touch and subtle breath creates the music that reaches the heavens. Each life has the potential to become a beautiful melody, a completely original composition and ultimately a song of praise to the Creator. Just like the ripples in a pond, the sounds that emanate from one life spread out and touch all of those around them. This story is simply the sheet music to one such melody and thus the title, "The Ballad of Billy Turner."

I. The Playground Exorcist

"Oh my God, it's little Billy Turner"! The realization hit me like a wave of ice water. I'm not sure how I didn't make the connection sooner. I mean, he really didn't look that much different than he did twenty five years ago. Of course, back then he was only 8 years old, but it was the same face with a grown-up body. After spending a lifetime in education, it wasn't unusual to encounter former students, though they always seemed to remember me better than I did them. But Billy Turner was a different story. My life was profoundly changed by that little boy's life and as I stared at the television screen the memories came flooding back to me.

My first real encounter with Billy was when I worked as the Guidance Counselor at an elementary school just outside of San Diego. I had minored in psychology in college, so after a few years of teaching I was happy to make the jump from the classroom, when the counselor position opened up. While I generally liked the kids, I found the day-to-day routine of teaching to be somewhat oppressive. Working with the kids in this new role was much more rewarding. Since there was only one counselor assigned to an elementary school, I tried to make sure that I knew who all the kids were and that they knew who I was too. After all, I didn't want to be "a stranger" if they ever needed help. I hung out on the playground during recess, in the hallways between classes, in the cafeteria at lunch, and I even quietly slipped into classes to observe periodically. I learned a lot more about the kids by watching them than I ever did by speaking directly to them. I could normally pick the ones whom I was likely to see in my office, so I wasn't all that surprised when the call came about Billy.

As I headed for Principal Skinner's office, I stopped by his secretary's desk to get the lowdown. Though I'd worked with him for a few years, I never sensed that he thought much of me and I wanted to be prepared. She told me that there had been "incident" on the playground involving Billy and another boy, Jared Lowe. She wasn't sure exactly what happened, but Jared's father had come to see Principal Skinner and was quite animated in his demands that action be taken. I imagined that this was probably just a typical scrape between two second grade boys, though it sounded like Billy must have gotten the upper hand, which was a little surprising. Jared was a pretty rough kid, bigger and more aggressive than Billy. But I pushed those thoughts aside as I entered the office, figuring I might as well just wait and hear what actually happened. With the benefit of twenty-five years of hindsight, I can now see how unprepared I was to deal with what came next.

Principal Mike Skinner was a highly respected man and somewhat of a rising star in the school district. Though he was only a few years older than I, he had already hop-scotched over several older and more experienced educators to become the principal. We all knew that he was likely to be moved up to the high school level before long, so I understood that he'd want to move swiftly to address whatever this issue was. As I entered his office I could see that he was genuinely troubled.

"Bob, please come in and sit down."

"Thanks Mike, what's happening?"

"Well, we've had a little incident that I need you to get involved in."

"I'll do what I can; tell me the story."

"Well, let me start by asking what you know about Billy Turner and Jared Lowe?"

For some reason this question stirred a feeling of insecurity in me and I unconsciously dodged it by answering, "Well, neither one of them has ever been in my office."

"I understand that, Bob, but I know that you watch these kids. I want you to tell me what you've seen."

The fact that he acknowledged that I did watch the kids made me feel a little better, though his tone definitely conveyed a sense of urgency. I tried to speak freely, saying, "I guess I'll start with Jared. It seems pretty clear to me that he's in a rough situation at home. He appears to have a lot of anger and spends most of his time alone. He's not really a bully, but he shows some pretty classic signs of abuse."

Before I could go on, Mike stopped me, saying, "OK, I get the picture. I don't really want to open up another can of worms with speculation about what's happening at home, so let's just say that he's a troubled kid."

Nodding, I hesitantly replied, "Yes, I believe he is a troubled kid."

"So what about Billy Turner?" he pressed.

"He's an interesting kid, almost the opposite of Jared. He's very outgoing and social, though I think that he comes on a little strong for the other kids. He's always around other people, but I don't sense that any of them feel close to him. When you talk to him he seems pretty bright, but I know that his teachers struggle to keep him focused, and I don't think that he's doing very well in the classroom."

"Do you have any sense of problems at home?"

"No, I'm not sure about his father, but I've seen his mother drop him off and pick him up every day. They seem very close. The kid doesn't seem to suffer from a lack of self confidence, so I assume someone is encouraging him."

"Have you seen anything to suggest a religious affiliation?"

I couldn't suppress a smile at that question, as I answered, "Oh yeah, Billy loves to talk about Jesus."

Mike seemed irritated that I found that somewhat amusing, as he sharply retorted, "Do you believe that he's trying to proselytize the other children?"

Proselytize seemed like an absurd term to use and I barely concealed my distain for it as I exclaimed, "Wow, I guess it's a little hard for me to associate that word with an eight year old."

My assertion seemed to further agitate him, as he tersely replied, "Well, you better expand your thinking, because that's at the heart of our issue here!"

I tried to back pedal a little, saying, "I'm sorry, I wasn't trying to say that it isn't a valid question. It just seems like a pretty strong word to use for a child who's excited about Jesus."

Mike's voice seemed to deepen as he petulantly said, "On a strictly personal level, I'd probably agree with you. I mean I went to Church camp and Vacation Bible School when I was a kid too. But the world has changed a lot since then and in my role as principal, my personal beliefs can't affect my judgment. Mr. Lowe feels like Billy's religious activity has infringed on his son's civil rights and he's threatening legal action if we don't do something about it."

Still struggling to see this as a big deal, I asked, "He's that upset that Billy talked to his son about Jesus?"

"Oh no, Billy did a lot more than talk about Jesus."

"What do you mean?" I asked blankly.

"According to Mr. Lowe, he tried to perform some sort of exorcism."

"What?" I gasped.

"Yes, he said that Billy told Jared that there was some sort of evil spirit on him and that he was going to cast it out; he says that Jared has been terrified ever since."

It occurred to me to look for a hidden camera, wondering whether this was some sort of twisted practical joke. Looking at Mike, I asked, "Are we sure that this isn't just a story that Jared has come up with?"

"I wish," Mike replied. "According to Mrs. Phillips, who broke the whole thing up on the playground, she found Billy with his hands on Jared's shoulders, alternately shouting to God and then at the devil, while Jared stood there crying and shaking like he'd just gotten out of the bathtub. When I talked to Billy, he didn't deny any of it. He genuinely seemed perplexed as to why any of this would be a problem."

"Oh my God," I exclaimed, as I realized he was serious about this.

Mike Skinner looked as close to worried as I'd ever seen him as he said, "Yeah, you can imagine how this will look if it gets out."

Nodding in agreement, I said, "I've never heard of anything like this. What is it that you think I'll be able to do?"

"Well, I'm not sure really, but I want you to start by performing a psychological evaluation of Billy."

The term "psychological evaluation" concerned me, as I reminded him, "You do realize that I'm not a licensed psychologist and that my evaluation wouldn't necessarily be accepted in a court case?"

"Of course, I know that, but depending on what you find, I'm hoping that we'll be able to avoid the whole court scene."

Genuinely perplexed, I asked, "I guess I don't follow you."

"All I'm saying is that if the kid has issues, maybe he doesn't belong in a regular classroom with other kids."

Not liking the sound of that, I queried, "What kind of issues are we talking about?"

"I don't know, you're the counselor; emotional issues, learning disabilities, whatever! I'm just saying that if we find something like that, maybe we can take some action that will satisfy Mr. Lowe and thereby avoid a courtroom drama."

I remember being shocked by what Mike seemed to be suggesting. After all I was pretty sure that Mr. Lowe was at the very least beating on his son, and Jared was certainly more of a problem student than Billy. It was almost as if he wanted me to find something wrong with him. I told him that I'd meet with Billy and that I'd have to involve his parents too. This seemed to satisfy Principal Skinner for the moment, but I could feel the weight on my shoulders as I returned to my office. I certainly couldn't defend what Billy had done, but it was impossible for me to ignore the fact that he was only eight years old.

As I pictured the scene in my mind, I couldn't suppress a smile. The wild eyed fanatic preacher, little Billy Turner, shouting to the heavens; rough and tough Jared Lowe, standing a full six inches taller than his assailant, shaking and crying like a baby.

The ever anxious Mrs. Phillips trying to wrestle them apart; it was like something from a bad movie. After that brief moment of amusement, the seriousness of the situation washed over me. I realized for the first time that part of what had made the counselor position so attractive to me, was the belief that I'd be able to avoid situations like this. Now I found myself right in the middle of a mess that I never could have imagined.

I was sitting at my desk, lost in my thoughts, when I became aware that someone was watching me. When I looked up, I found that Billy was standing in my doorway, staring intently at me. His eyes seemed fixed and unmoved by the fact that I was now looking back at him; somehow I found it disconcerting. It wasn't until I spoke to him that he finally moved.

"Can I help you?"

"Oh, yes sir, I'm Billy Turner and my teacher said that I should come see you."

"Well, come in Billy; sit right over here."

"OK," he chirped.

"Do you know who I am Billy?"

"Yes Sir, you're Mr. Davis, the school counselor."

"Do you know what a counselor does?"

"No sir."

"Well, a counselor helps people with their problems."

"You mean like with math problems?" he asked sincerely.

I couldn't help but smile, as I replied, "Well, not exactly; we try to help people who are sad, or afraid, or in trouble."

"Oh, so that's why I'm here," he said knowingly.

"What do you mean, Billy?"

"Because I'm in trouble for praying for Jared."

Wanting to put his mind at ease, I said, "Well, I want you to understand that you're not in trouble with me Billy, but we do need to talk about what happened with Jared."

"OK," he enthusiastically replied.

"So, tell me, are you and Jared friends?"

"Not really. Jared isn't friends with anybody."

"Why do you think Jared doesn't have many friends?"

"You mean *any*," Billy said.

"*Any* what?" I asked.

"*Any* friends," he said emphatically

"OK, *any* friends," I conceded.

"Because he's mean!" he said.

"How is he mean?" I prodded.

"He won't talk to anyone, or play with them, or anything. If you try to be nice to him, he says mean stuff back to you."

"Have you tried to be nice to him?" I asked.

"Sure, the Bible says that we should be nice to everyone, even people who won't be nice back to us."

"What did he say when you've tried to be nice to him?"

Billy's face twisted slightly as he replied, "He called me a loser."

"Did that make you mad?" I continued.

"Yeah, it did, but I know I'm not supposed to get into fights, so I just tried to stay away from him."

Though I'd already heard the story, I wanted to hear Billy tell it, so I asked, "So, what made you go to him on the playground the other day?"

"When I saw him standing all by himself I felt like the Lord told me to go pray for him," he replied innocently.

A little internal alarm went off in my head as I tried to process Billy's words. I wondered if these were the same words he'd used with Principal Skinner. Wanting to clarify, I asked, "Do you mean that you felt sorry for him and thought that God would want you to pray for him, or do you mean that you felt like God actually spoke to you?"

"Both," he said. "I figured that God wanted me to pray for him because He told me so."

I could suddenly understand Mike Skinner's anxiety, as I continued, "Do you hear from God often?"

"Everyday!" he said cheerfully.

"Really, when was the last time that you felt like you heard from Him?" I asked cautiously.

"Just now, when I got to your office," he replied.

"Really, and what did He say?"

"He said that you were a nice man and that I didn't need to be afraid."

"Well, that's good. Why do you think that God talks to you?"

"Because He loves me," he replied with a grin.

I guess I should've seen that one coming and I looked for ways to rephrase the question. "Yeah, but He loves everybody doesn't He?"

"Sure," Billy nodded.

"But, He doesn't talk to everybody," I added.

"My Mom says that He talks to everyone who believes in Him," he replied sweetly.

"Really, well, I believe in Him and He doesn't talk to me?" I said incredulously.

"You know, there's lots of times that my Mom talks to me and I don't hear her because I'm not really listening. Maybe that's what's happening with you and God," he replied in a some-what patronizing tone.

My irritation with that theory spilled out, as I said, "I'm pretty sure that if God were speaking to me I'd know it."

"Do you believe in Jesus?" Billy prodded.

"Billy, I already told you that I believed in God, and besides, it's my job to ask the questions," I answered in an exasperated voice.

"Oh, sorry," he asserted.

Not willing to let go of the point, I decided to give Billy a little test, saying, "That's alright; do you think if you asked God, that He would say something to you right now?"

"Probably," he said.

"Can you give that a try?" I asked in a soft voice.

"OK."

As Billy closed his eyes and began to rock back and forth in his chair, a wave of panic came over me. I suddenly realized that in my curiosity I had invited this boy to pray in my office and that the door was standing wide open. I jumped from my chair and quickly closed it. As I made my way back to the desk, I caught myself staring at this child. Part of me knew that what he was saying was totally absurd, but another part of me almost wondered if he knew something that I didn't. I had been raised in church, but never met anyone who claimed to hear God's voice before. After another couple of minutes of swaying and mumbling something beneath his breath, Billy's eyes opened suddenly and he sat perfectly still. He looked at me in a way that no child ever has and for a second it felt as though he were looking through me. When the moment passed, he relaxed and once again took on the countenance of a little boy.

"So, did you hear from Him?" I asked.

"Yup," he replied.

"And what did He say?"

"Well, He didn't really speak; He gave me a vision."

Another little internal alarm went off inside my head, as the plot continued to thicken. "A vision?" I asked.

"Yeah, it's like a dream, but you're not really asleep," he said.

"I know what a vision is," I said impatiently. "Does God normally give you visions?"

"Sometimes," he replied.

"Well, tell me about your vision?" I asked skeptically.

"It was about you!" he said.

"Me?"

"Yes, you were standing in a river and you were helping this dark haired lady get through the water."

"Really, was there anything else?" I queried.

"Yeah, you were holding a baby," he added.

"A baby? Did God explain this vision to you?" I queried.

"Nope."

"Then how do you know what it means?"

"I think it means that this is going to happen to you."

"You mean like it's telling me the future?" I asked.

"Yeah, I guess."

I decided to stop for a minute, because I could see that I was getting nowhere. It had been risky to try something like this and I was really beginning to regret that I'd taken this direction. If it got back to a teacher or Principal Skinner, I could be in real trouble. I decided that I'd better get back to the real issue and to see what else I could find out.

"So, tell me Billy, when you got to Jared, what did you say?"

"I told him that He had a big demon on his back and that I would make it go away if he wanted me to."

By this point, my internal alarm system was pretty much overloaded. First, God's voice, then visions and now demons. I had to admit that Billy had an incredible imagination, but this story wouldn't play very well in a courtroom. I tried to keep things on track by asking, "But I thought you went over to pray for him?"

"I did, but when I got close to him I could hear that thing talking to him."

"You could hear 'what thing' talking to him?" I pressed.

Billy expression curled, as though that was a dumb question, "The demon on his back."

"So you could hear the 'demon' speaking; do you hear demons often?"

"No, not much, but I have heard them before."

"Really, and that didn't scare you?"

"No, I'm a child of the King; no hairy demon can mess with me!" he said confidently.

I caught myself staring at Billy; wondering whether he was a kid with some sort of special spiritual ability or just an eight year old boy with an over-active imagination. Unfortunately, I had to play the hand I was dealt, so I asked, "What exactly was the demon saying?"

"He was telling Jared that he ought to kill his mom and dad," Billy said seriously.

"Really!"

"Yeah, I had this vision of them in a burning house," he went on.

"Did that scare you?" I asked.

"Yes, Sir, it did."

"So what did Jared say to you?"

"He said to get away, but I figured that it was just that old demon talking, so I decided that I was going to get rid of that thing."

"So you started to pray?"

"Yup, I came against it in Jesus' name!" he said with a smile.

"And what happened then?"

"Well, that thing started growlin' and howlin' and doin' all the crazy stuff that demons do, but I kept coming against it in the name of Jesus."

Again, the picture in my mind was almost laughable, but this time I managed to suppress the smile. "What was Jared doing?"

"Well, he was the one howlin' and growlin', cause that thing had him."

"So, what happened then?"

"Well, Mrs. Phillips came and tried to break us up."

"Did you stop?" I asked.

"No, that demon wasn't gone yet. I figured that Mrs. Phillips didn't really understand what I was doing, so I just finished it," he said confidently.

"Finished it?" I prodded.

"Yeah, that thing finally let go with a scream and it was gone!" he replied.

"You mean that you made the demon go?"

"No, it wasn't me, it was Jesus that made it go."

"So, Jared was better when you were done?"

"He was crying and stuff, but I figured that he must be glad to have that demon off his back."

"Have you talked to Jared since then?" I continued.

"No, sir, they told me to stay away from him."

"And you've done that?"

"Yes, sir."

I decided that I'd heard enough and after coaching Billy about the confidential nature of our conversations, I sent him back to class. I was deeply disturbed by what I'd seen and heard. I'm not sure which I feared worse, that Billy was completely delusional or that maybe he wasn't. Certainly a kid who hears voices and takes action based on what they say, is a problem, but it was hard to imagine that Billy posed any real threat to the other kids. I tried hard to let myself be open to the idea that maybe there was something legitimate about Billy. After all he seemed very sincere. But there was just no way for a rational person to buy into the idea of God speaking to an eight year old boy or using him to dispose of evil spirits on the playground.

As I replayed the conversation in my mind, I remembered the supposed vision, which really didn't make any sense. There wasn't a river within fifty miles, my wife had blonde hair and we had no children. I couldn't conjure a scenario that could possibly validate that picture. As I flipped the facts over in my mind, I could find no plausible defense for Billy Turner. While the fact that he was a little boy with a big imagination would account for a certain amount of irrational behavior, it wasn't enough to cover the whole thing. I had to admit that this kid had a head full of voices and that his willingness to act on them made him a wild card. I suppose that I should've been pleased, after all, Principal Skinner would be happy to hear of Billy's potentially schizophrenic tendencies. But I just couldn't shake the feeling that I needed to keep digging. One thing that I knew for sure was that I wasn't ready to talk about it. Unfortunately for me, Principal Skinner was, and when I looked up, he was standing in my doorway.

"So, how did it go?" he asked.

"Well, it's hard to say, we only had a few minutes to talk," I responded weakly.

"But what did he tell you?"

"He pretty much confirmed what you already told me."

"Pretty much? Come on Bob, what is it that you don't want to say?" he pressed.

I tried to evade by saying, "I don't know, I'd just like to talk to Jared to get his side of things."

I could see the irritation rising in him, as he sharply asked, "I don't understand why. The accounts that I got from Mrs. Phillips and Mr. Lowe have already been confirmed by Billy. What is it that you want to hear from Jared?"

"I don't know. I just want to hear what was going on in his head at the time," I shot back in a tone that gave away my own agitation.

Principal Skinner's face was flush, as his tone rose up to meet mine, "I can't see how that really matters. The pertinent question is what was going on in Billy Turner's head. So, now that you've spoken to him you should have some sort of answer to that question. That is what we're paying you for, right?"

"Yes," I replied indignantly, "That is what you're paying me for. I just want to make sure I've got the full picture before I make any sort of judgments."

Still angry, he fired back, "Well, that's fine, Bob, but as the principal of this school I have an obligation to the students and the parents to make sure that this issue is addressed promptly. So I need you to tell me what you derived from your interview with Billy."

I knew that I couldn't avoid telling him what Billy had said and finally sputtered, "He hears voices."

"What? What kind of voices?"

"He believes that he hears God's voice," I offered.

"You said *voices*, plural; what other *voices* are we talking about?" he asked with a sparkle in his eyes.

"Demons," I mumbled.

"Demons!" Mike gasped.

"That's what he said," I replied.

"So, this kid is walking around with a head full of voices and arbitrarily acting on what they tell him?"

"I'm not sure that I'd say arbitrarily."

"Come on Bob, are you ready to make the argument that this kid can tell the good voices from the bad voices?"

"No, I'm not ready to make any argument. Like I said before, I need more time to look into this."

"Well, you can keep looking, but based on what you've already told me, I've got to get this boy out of the classroom," Mike said smugly.

"Come on Mike, do you really think this kid poses some sort of danger to the other kids?"

"Who can say for sure, what he's already done has got people upset. What happens if one of the voices tells him to bring a gun to school?"

"We haven't heard anything that would suggest that kind of

thing."

"Can you guarantee me that we won't? You're not the one who'll stand before the cameras, answering the press as they probe how the school administration was aware of this kid's issues and didn't take stronger action to protect the other students. While you may feel like this is all happening too fast, from my perspective we're already late!"

I knew not to continue this conversation with Mike. His mind was clearly set on what needed to happen and there was nothing I could say that was going to change that. Truthfully, I wasn't sure that I didn't agree with him. I just hated the sense that this outcome had been predetermined. I realized that my reluctance to share what I'd heard, and the perception that I might be defending Billy, had likely done damage to my credibility. I also understood that he, and the rest of the school's administration, would heavily scrutinize whatever conclusion I reached in the end. I could see that how I handled this situation was likely to significantly impact my future in the education system.

Mike let me know that he was placing Billy on suspension pending the outcome of our inquiry, and he left it up to me to contact his parents. Not surprisingly, Mike volunteered to call Mr. Lowe to inform him of our intended action. By the time he left my office it was already after 4:00 p.m., and I knew I'd be forced to call Billy's parents at home. Given Billy's level of religious zeal I imagined that his parents would be downright fanatical, so I braced myself for the inevitable hostile reaction as I dialed the phone.

Mrs. Turner answered the phone, and after a brief introduction, I asked if she was aware of the incident on the playground. In a very calm voice she let me know that Billy had let her know about it and that she'd also received a note from his home room teacher. I informed her that I had discussed the situation with Billy, and that I very much wanted the opportunity to speak to her and her husband. She informed me that she was scheduled to work the following day, but that she could probably make arrangements to have someone cover for her. She also let me know that Billy's father wouldn't be available. I took a deep breath before finally letting her know that Billy was officially suspended from school until this issue was completely resolved. After a momentary pause, she quietly said, "I understand."

Trying not to convey my surprise, I let her know that we'd have Billy's books and assignments ready for her when she came for the meeting and that I'd see her the following day. After I hung up the phone, I sat in shocked relief at the lack of hostility from Mrs. Turner, though part of me wondered if this wasn't just the calm before the storm. As I gathered my things to head home I heard the sound of thunder outside. Despite the fact that rain was in the forecast I couldn't shake the feeling that this was some sort of bad omen. I forced myself to write down some notes from the conversation that I'd had with Billy, knowing that if Mr. Lowe didn't take us to court, Billy's parents probably would. By the time I got to my car, the parking lot was empty and the rain had started to fall.

II. Severe Weather

Because we got so little rain, I didn't even own an umbrella and was dripping by the time I got the car door closed. I was so preoccupied with thoughts about this situation that I was half way home before I remembered the "Open House" at my wife's office. She worked for an upscale real estate agency across town, and they were doing their quarterly "meet and greet" with prominent business people from the community. Claire was sure to be agitated by the fact that I was running so late and that I hadn't called. Truthfully, I dreaded these things, and she knew it, but I honestly had just forgotten this one. She always claimed that I wasn't supportive of her career, which seemed ironic to me. I had been the one who suggested that she try real estate in the first place, I'd paid for the school, and I'd agreed to put off having a family so that she could pursue her career. I'd even bought her a much nicer car than we could really afford, so that she could drive clients around. I'm not sure what else I could have done to be supportive, but apparently it wasn't enough.

As I got within a couple of blocks of the office, I could see that there was no place to park. It was probably just as well, as Claire didn't like me to park my car (which was rusting and falling apart) where people could see it. Of course, by the time I walked three blocks in the rain I was soaking wet. As I stepped into the foyer of the crowded office I heard several of Claire's co-workers shout, "Bob!", followed by several less than funny comments about how wet I was. I tried to smile and laugh it off, but I knew what was coming.

Sure enough, within seconds I saw Claire glaring at me from across the room and I shrugged in an attempt to apologize.

She just shook her head and went back to her conversation. After spending some time in the restroom trying to straighten up, I made my way to her side. She ignored my presence until she was done charming yet another potential customer and then she motioned me toward her office. Even though she had closed the door, she spoke in an angry whisper.

"It's nice that you could make it, Bob," she hissed through clinched teeth.

"I'm really sorry, Claire, I got held up at work and then there was the rain."

"Of course you'd pick a day when we're doing Open House to work late. I suppose the rain knocked out telephone service to the school?" she shot back.

"Of course not, I just got wrapped up in a situation with a student and lost track of things."

"Well, excuse me if the timing of your little situation strikes me as somewhat convenient. If I knew that you were going to come in here this late and looking like that, I'd have told you not to bother."

Feeling as though I'd already been through the grinder with Mike Skinner, I was in no mood for this exchange, as I cynically replied, "Well, I never knew attendance was optional."

"Oh yeah, like I ask so much of you; you can't even come and support me once a quarter?"

"I'm here, aren't I? Come on, Claire; is this really what you want to do?"

"No, but you're going to have a hard time convincing me that you didn't do this on purpose."

"Well, I can promise you that I didn't, so let's just get back out there and make the most of the time you've got left."

"Fine," she huffed.

When she opened the door, a warm smile spilled across her face, as she stepped back into action. I dutifully followed her for the next ninety minutes, smiling, nodding, and listening to an endless river of small talk. Over the years I'd developed the ability to listen just enough to know when to nod and smile. At the same time that I was feigning interest, I was brooding over the fate of Billy Turner. On a purely intellectual level I couldn't justify him, but something inside of me kept pushing me into his corner. I hadn't really thought deeply about God in years, and I certainly never believed in the kind of things that Billy talked about. But why was it so wrong for a little boy to believe that God might speak to him or that he'd want to help someone who he thought was in trouble? It was confusing, and it was beginning to get under my skin. By the time we got home I really needed to talk about it. Unfortunately Claire was not in the best of moods. After telling her the whole story, she just stared at me.

"So, what exactly is the problem?" she asked.

"I'm just afraid that we're being too hasty with this kid," I replied.

"I'm sorry, Babe, but I just don't see it. This kid sounds like some sort of religious fanatic," she said coldly.

"He's just a little kid, and what's so wrong with him believing in God?" I offered.

"Come on, Bob, you watch the news. How many times have we seen people shoot abortion doctors or drown their kids, or murder their parents, and then say that God told them to do it? Maybe you're reliving some fond childhood memory of Sunday school, but the reality is that these religious fanatics are killing this country and now they're starting to indoctrinate their kids, too. I've got to go with Skinner on this one. You need to get this kid out of there and send a message to all the other religious nuts!"

"All I want is to make sure that this kid gets treated fairly," I said.

"What's not fair about any of this? No one is putting words in the kid's mouth; you're just repeating what he said. The kid hears voices and has visions and sees demons. I mean, what else is it that you need to hear?"

That sounded eerily close to what Principal Skinner had said, and it was hard not to agree. Still, I couldn't shake a nagging sense of doubt, as I said, "I don't know, I just can't help but think that this kid isn't the big threat we're making him out to be."

"Look, Bob, I love that you've got a heart for these kids, but you better take a hard look at this one. Trying to defend this kid could cost you your career, and it's a little late for you to be starting over again," she said, as she pulled the sheet over her.

Claire's words echoed in my ears. Even though I'd already realized the potential career implications, hearing her say it out loud seemed to bring on a stark sense of reality. In that moment it was clear to me that I didn't really have an option and that ultimately she was right. We weren't putting words into Billy's mouth or adding anything to his story. All I had to do was to accurately report the facts and let the administration make their decision.

After a few minutes, I moved over to kiss Claire goodnight and realized that she had already fallen asleep. I turned out the light and lay there listening to the rain and to the faint sound of thunder. I thought about how happy she'd once seemed, and I wondered at what had happened. As I poured through the memories, it dawned on me that her excitement was always more centered on the idea of building a new life than on the idea of being with me. Buying a house, having careers, raising our social standing; those are the things that seemed to fire Claire's passion. Certainly, I couldn't recall a time when she was particularly passionate for me, but I guess I'd just tried to convince myself that being excited about our life together was the same thing. Anymore, it seemed as though my mere presence annoyed her, and I suddenly felt humiliated as I pondered how pitiful I must seem to her.

It was oddly similar to the feeling I'd had earlier as I talked to Billy about God. Part of me wanted to defend my position and yet, a bigger part of me felt like a phony. How could I claim to be Claire's partner when there didn't seem to be any genuine passion between us, and how could I claim to know God when I'd never heard His voice? It was as though I were some kind of amnesia patient, waking up and wondering who I really was. Though I continued to wrestle with these thoughts, for what seemed to be hours, I eventually succumbed to the sound of the rain and fell into a fitful sleep.

While falling asleep to the sound of the rain had been somewhat soothing, waking up to the sound of it was almost impossible. I just couldn't seem to clear the cobwebs from my head and, after about the fourth time I hit the snooze, I could hear Claire growling. I dragged myself into the shower and was running late by the time I got to office. The rain showed no signs of letting up, and though I'd managed to stay pretty dry by draping a windbreaker over my head, my socks were soaked from the deep puddles that had formed in the parking lot.

As soon as I got a cup of coffee I sent for Jared Lowe. I wanted to talk to him before I spoke to Mrs. Turner, who wasn't due to arrive until later in the morning. A few minutes later, Jared stood in my doorway, seemingly unable to look me in the eye or to speak above a mumble.

"Please, Jared, come in and sit down," I said.

"OK," he murmured.

"Do you know who I am, Jared?"

With his eyes downcast, he answered, "Yeah."

"And do you know why you're here?"

"No."

In just a few short questions, it was clear that the difference between a conversation with Billy and one with Jared was going to be like night and day.

"I want to talk to you about Billy Turner and what happened on the playground," I continued.

"OK."

"Are you and Billy friends?" I prodded.

"No."

"Do you know who Billy is?"

"Yes."

"Do you consider Billy your enemy?"

"No."

"So, he's not your friend or your enemy; what would you call him?" I asked.

Jared's eyes briefly rose to meet mine, as he answered, "Annoying."

Sensing his first hint of emotion, I pressed on. "How is he annoying, Jared?"

"He talks too much."

"Is there anything else?"

"Yes, he talks too much about Jesus."

"Do you believe in Jesus, Jared?"

"We're not church people," he replied evasively.

"That's not what I asked. I asked if you believed in Jesus."

"I suppose," he said with a shrug.

"So why does Billy's talking about Jesus bother you?"

Again making brief eye contact, he said, "Because he never stops, it's like that's all he knows about."

"On the day that he came to you on the playground, what were you doing?" I asked.

"I was thinking."

"Can you remember what you were thinking about, Jared?"

"Yeah, I was thinking about my parents."

"What were you thinking about your parents, Jared?"

"How much I hate them," he said as he stared at the floor.

"Enough to wish that they were dead?" I queried.

I knew that I had no business asking that question, but I couldn't resist the temptation. Jared raised his head and looked me right in the eye and said, "Sometimes." I was dumbfounded by how easily he'd answered the question and how little remorse he seemed to have at his response. I tried to regain my composure so that I could continue.

"What did you think when Billy walked up to you and said he wanted to pray for you?"

"I thought he was nuts."

"So why didn't you just make him go away?"

"I couldn't," he replied with a puzzled look.

"I don't understand, Jared, you're much bigger and stronger. Why couldn't you make him leave you alone?" I asked.

"I don't know. It was the weirdest thing. He was looking at me real funny, and I just couldn't seem to stop him."

"Did you try to stop him?"

"I remember thinking that I kind of wanted him to stop."

"You 'kind of' wanted him to stop," I prodded.

"Yeah, it was kind of confusing because part of me didn't want him to stop."

"So what happened?"

"I just stood there and he went nuts, yelling and shaking and stuff."

"Did you feel anything?"

"Yeah, I felt like my guts were gonna explode and like I was going to puke all over him."

"So then what happened?"

"Mrs. Phillips came up and tried to stop him, but Billy kept going."

"So what finally caused Billy to stop?"

"Something happened and then he just stopped," Jared replied.

"What do you mean that something happened?"

"I don't know, it's like something popped inside of me and then he just stopped."

"Did you feel any different after that?"

"I guess," he said.

"How did you feel different?"

"I don't know, calm I guess. I'd normally punch anyone who grabbed me like that, but I really wasn't mad when he stopped."

"Did you talk to Billy?"

"No, they drug him off to the office, and I haven't talked to him since. I heard he got suspended."

"So has all of this bothered you?" I asked.

"Not really," he said.

"It hasn't given you bad dreams or anything?"

"No way. It's kind of weird, but I still feel real calm."

I gave Jared the same confidentiality speech I'd given Billy, and I sent him back to class. I'd been disturbed by what Billy had said to me, but I was positively shaken by my conversation with Jared. It certainly reinforced my sense that Mr. and maybe even Mrs. Lowe were abusing their son. Nine year old boys generally don't want to see their parents dead unless they're suffering at their hands. It also validated my suspicion that Mr. Lowe wasn't really interested in the trauma that his son might have experienced, but that he just wanted to exploit this situation. Of course, the most surprising thing about the conversation was that it completely corroborated Billy's story about sensing that Jared wanted to kill his parents, and that he'd successfully exorcised some foul spirit. I was totally unprepared for that, and I began to get a sick feeling in my stomach.

I felt like I was in a pressure cooker, with Mike Skinner on one side, pressing me to declare this boy "too dangerous to be around the other kids." The deceptive Mr. Lowe on another side, making accusations to distract us from his own guilt, and little Billy Turner on yet another side innocently asking, "Mr. Davis, do you believe in Jesus?" Of course, there was also my wife, wagging her finger at me and warning me that my career was at stake. And as if all of that wasn't enough, I realized that somewhere in the midst of all this was God Himself, challenging me about what I really believed. My head began to throb, as I stared out my window at what seemed to be a never ending rain.

III. Voices

Promptly at 10:00 am, Mrs. Turner arrived at my office. Though I'd seen her from a distance before, she seemed younger and more attractive close-up. She was a slim and somewhat petite woman, with bright eyes and a warm smile. Given the circumstances, she was surprisingly composed. After introducing myself, I took some time to review the facts with her to ensure that she'd heard the same story. After she confirmed that this was the same thing that Billy had told her, I found myself wanting to hear her perspective on the incident.

"Mrs. Turner, the father of the boy that Billy was trying to 'help' has come to the school's administration and would like to see some kind of action taken. He feels that Billy's actions were inappropriate and detrimental to his son. I would be interested in hearing your thoughts on how we might respond to his concerns."

"Well, I certainly cannot deny that it was totally inappropriate," she replied.

"Really, so you don't approve of what Billy did?"

"I don't think that it is appropriate for someone Billy's age to even attempt such a thing; much less with another child, who has no understanding of what is going on, and certainly not on the playground at school."

I exhaled some of the tension that had built up in me about our conversation as I said, "I guess I'm relieved to hear you say that."

"I can assure you, Mr. Davis, I've discussed this with Billy, and I feel certain that this sort of thing won't happen again. I'm certainly willing to sit down with this boy's parents and to give them that same assurance," she continued.

"I appreciate that, Mrs. Turner, but I'm not sure that it's that simple. You see, in the course of my interview with Billy, he said some things that are a cause for concern, and we really need to address those things before we can completely resolve this issue."

I could see the concern in her expression as she asked, "What sort of things are we talking about, Mr. Davis?"

"Well, Billy mentioned hearing voices... voices that weren't necessarily his own," I said carefully.

"Do you mean God's voice?" she said.

"Well, yes, amongst others," I replied.

"Mr. Davis, are you a Christian person?"

"Yes, Mrs. Turner, I was raised in church."

"Did the church that you grew up in believe in the Bible?"

"Of course, what kind of Christian church doesn't?" I replied.

"You might be surprised by what passes for Christian these days, but assuming that you hold the Bible as the source for truth, then we probably don't need to get into that. In the scripture it says that we who believe are His sheep and that His sheep know His voice. Billy is one of His sheep and He knows the voice of the Good Shepherd," she answered.

"I am certainly familiar with the metaphor of the Good Shepherd and His sheep, but do you really believe that was meant to be viewed literally?"

"Yes, I do think that is how it was meant to be viewed, but for the sake of our discussion, how does it change if we view it metaphorically? We still have the Good Shepherd, Jesus, communicating with His sheep, which are those who follow Him, and them being able to distinguish that communication."

I couldn't help but be impressed with her answer. Though I got the sense that neither of us really wanted to have this conversation, I found her words to be thought provoking and her demeanor to be engaging. Not really knowing how to respond, I stammered, "Well, OK, but do you really think that it's an audible voice?"

"It doesn't really matter whether it is an audible voice, or an inner voice, or a vision, or even a dream. It is still the Shepherd communicating with His sheep," she added.

I caught my mind drifting from the incident to this idea of God speaking and I found myself wanting to hear more about that, so I said, "Billy mentioned that you'd taught him that all believers hear God's voice, but I was raised as a Christian, and I certainly have never heard Him speak."

"Mr. Davis, I cannot speak directly to your experience, but I can promise you that if you belong to Him, He's spoken to you, whether you've understood it or not," she stated definitively.

Feeling suddenly defensive, I said, "I think that we're probably getting off the subject here."

Mrs. Turner's glance almost seemed to pierce me, as she said, "I'm sorry to disagree with you, but it seems to me that whether my son legitimately hears the voice of God is at the very heart of the issue. How you view this subject will likely make all of the difference in what comes next for him."

"OK, I do see your point, but my experience isn't really pertinent," I grumbled.

"With all due respect, Sir, you were willing to contradict what I've taught my son based on your experience, and it was you who interjected that experience into our conversation. As I said previously, I cannot speak to your experience, but if you are willing to concede that it may not be pertinent, then I'd suggest that just because you've never recognized the voice of God, doesn't mean that He doesn't speak or that there aren't people who can distinguish that voice."

I was again impressed by her clarity of thought and I sensed that I was a little over my head in this conversation. I wouldn't have claimed to know much about spiritual things, and Mrs. Turner seemed to be something of an authority. Wanting to shift the topic from "God's voice," I said, "OK, for the sake of argument, let's just suppose that I buy into the idea that Billy hears God's voice. How do I explain his claim to hear the voices of, and for that matter, to see, demons?"

"Again, Mr. Davis, these things are discussed in the Bible. Billy is a very special boy, to whom God has given special abilities. God exists in the spiritual realm, and because we were made in His image, we too, are spiritual. God has given Billy a special awareness of that realm; he hears and sees things that other people cannot. I understand that within your profession that may be difficult to put into context, but that doesn't make it any less real. I certainly didn't grow up believing in all of this, and no one has ever really been able to explain it to me. But the last eight years with Billy have shown me the absolute reality of it."

"I guess the dilemma for me is that, even if I were to agree with what you're saying, how could I possibly make such a case to the school administration?" I asked.

"You can't," she said calmly.

"Excuse me?" I stammered.

"You can't convince them of such a thing, because to those who are perishing the cross is foolishness and spiritual things are spiritually discerned," she replied.

Feeling confused, I asked, "Which means… what?"

"Which means that you can't make people believe in something that they're not willing to see," she exclaimed.

"So where does that leave Billy?" I asked.

"In the hands of God, where he's always been," she said with resignation.

I found myself trying to interpret what she'd just said, because it almost sounded as if she was saying that I couldn't really defend Billy. I felt certain that couldn't be right, so I said, "Ma'am, I appreciate that you are a person of faith, but what exactly am I supposed to do for Billy?"

"Mr. Davis, all you can do is to be as honest and fair as possible. There really isn't any disagreement about what happened, the problem lies in deciding what it all means. People are going to think whatever they choose to think, but I believe that ultimately God will have His way," she replied.

"I admire your confidence, but aren't you worried about Billy being hurt by all of this?" I asked.

"Sir, there is nothing that I wouldn't do for my son, but I know very well that I can't control everything that goes on in his life. I believe that God has given Billy special abilities, because there is a special calling on his life; and I believe that facing adversity is an inherent part of his preparation. The Bible says that Jesus learned obedience from the things that He suffered, and if that was necessary for the preparation of God's own Son, I assume that it will be necessary for my son as well. My confidence is in the fact that God is faithful to complete the good work that He's already begun in Billy, and that He didn't stake anything on my perfection as a parent or your perfection as a counselor."

"Well, I hope that you're right about that," I concluded.

I took some time to show Mrs. Turner the materials that we were sending home for Billy, and she seemed to understand exactly what was needed. I couldn't help but be amazed by this woman. Despite what seemed to be some extreme philosophies about life, she was one of the most reasonable and articulate people that I'd ever talked to. Something in the way she presented herself made me feel as though her perspective was somehow more reasonable than my own. It seemed as though God was very tangible to her and I caught myself wanting to ask her more questions, but I recognized that this wasn't the time or the place. As she was about to leave my office, she turned and looked right into my eyes. It was the same knowing look that Billy had given me, and it made me feel like a little boy. With our eyes still locked together, a question spilled out of my mouth, in a voice so small that I could barely recognize it.

"What does God's voice sound like?"

"To you, it will sound just like your own voice," she replied.

"I don't understand," I stammered.

"God communicates through our spirit, and because of this, His voice comes through our being. That means that what He says often just seems like one of our own thoughts. This is why people generally don't recognize that He's speaking to them. Your enemy speaks to you in much the same way."

"How can you tell the difference between your own thoughts, the voice of God, and these other voices?" I asked.

"His Spirit dwells within everyone who believes in Him, and He bears witness to every word that He says," she declared.

"I don't understand," I replied.

"Something tells me that you will," she said confidently.

I had many more questions, but when I snapped out of my daze, Mrs. Turner was gone. I felt like I had dreamed that last part, and I sincerely wondered if it had actually happened or whether I'd somehow imagined it. There was something surreal about that whole exchange, and yet, I had a sense that I'd just experienced something profound. My head was swimming with all of the scenes and dialogues of the last couple of days. I wasn't only confused about what to do about this situation, I felt confused about who I was, what I really wanted, and even what I believed. I tried to narrow my focus back to the issue at hand, but my mind kept drifting back to the things that Mrs. Turner had been saying.

I caught myself trying to remember thoughts that I'd had, wondering if any of them had been God speaking to me. I wondered if His Holy Spirit lived in me, and if He did, why I never sensed that. I wondered if I was really one of "His sheep". And what of Billy's visions? After all, I could envision things in my mind's eye. Is that what they called a "vision" or was it some sort of out-of-body experience? I wondered how anyone could be sure of where the line between spiritual insight and active imagination should be drawn. Even though our meeting was finished in time for lunch, I didn't feel much like eating, and I spent the rest of the day sitting at my desk, lost in my thoughts.

IV. High Tide

As I walked to my car, the rain seemed to wake me up a little, and as I pulled out of the parking lot I turned on a Sports Talk show, hoping to give my mind a break. It had now been raining for over 24 hours and the sewer system was too overwhelmed to take any more water. Drainage from the gutters was overflowing onto the streets and, in places, onto the sidewalks. My little rust bucket of a car was struggling to make it through the flooding, with the tires frequently losing traction. Other drivers seemed to struggling as well, swerving to miss swells of water or hydroplaning when trying to stop. I tried to keep a safe distance from the other cars, but, invariably, they would decide to go around me.

As I approached a big intersection by the mall, I saw water shooting out of a huge culvert that passed under the road, as the overwhelmed drainage ditch tried to contain the excess. It was spectacular to look at, but I suddenly realized that the traffic directly in front of me had stopped, and I locked up the brakes. The tires slid effortlessly atop a layer of water, as I careened into the car stopped in front of me. Despite the fact that I wasn't really traveling very fast, the collision seemed violent. It took a few seconds to figure out that I was not seriously injured and to become aware of my surroundings again.

As I got out of the car, it occurred to me to check behind me for traffic. When I did this, I saw a small car sliding sideways toward my rear bumper. I immediately spun around, bracing myself for the impact. But after a few long seconds, it was clear that the car had somehow missed me. Oddly, when I checked behind me, the car was gone. Still in a daze from the

Bryan Corbin

impact, I got out of my car and began to look around. Suddenly I realized that the little car that had been sliding up behind me had gone off the road and into the flooded drainage ditch. I could see that the water was up over its hood, and the passenger compartment appeared to filling up with water. I could also see that the passenger within the vehicle was in a panic. Without thinking, I ran toward the car, not really knowing what I was going to do when I got there.

As I waded into the rushing water, I was surprised by how powerful the current was. When the water reached waist level I had to grab the car door handle to avoid being swept away, and, even then, it felt as though the car itself might start to flow downstream. I could see that the driver had moved to the back seat, which was still above the water level, and appeared to be trying to push the back door open. The sound of the moving water was surprisingly loud, as I tried to shout directions to the person in the car. I continued to struggle against the current, with my feet braced against the back tire and my hands on the front door handle. The passenger in the car still seemed to be wrestling with something in the backseat, and water repeatedly filled my mouth as I tried to yell for her to open the back window. The car felt very unstable, as though it might be swept away at any moment, and I was fighting my own urge to panic.

Suddenly the back window started to come down, and I could hear the passenger screaming for help. I yelled for her to calm down and to get the window fully lowered. As she did that, water began pouring into the open window, and the car began to shift beneath us. Though it only moved a few feet, a fresh shot of adrenaline kicked in and the woman in the car began screaming, "My baby, my baby!" Again, I yelled for her to calm down and told her to pass her baby out to me. As she tried to hand the baby out of the window, I realized that I couldn't hold onto the child without letting go of the door handle and being swept down stream. I yelled for her to hold the baby against her chest and to come out of the window head first and facing upward. She held the infant tightly with one hand and grabbed the top of the window frame with the other. Once again the car started to move, and again, she began screaming. As she thrust her body through the window opening, the current seemed to grab a hold of her, pulling both her and the baby free from the car. As she flailed to keep the baby's head above the water, I let go of the door handle and lunged to grab her. I caught one of her ankles, which pulled both her and the baby under the water. I fought furiously to get my arms around her waist so that I could try to keep their faces out of the water, but everything I did seemed to pull them down even more. It momentarily occurred to me to let them go, but the sense that I needed to hold on was even stronger, and so I continued to struggle.

Just as I was able to get both of my arms around her, it felt as though we were sucked down into a whirlpool that seemed to go deeper than the drainage ditch could possibly have gone, but after only a few seconds in this liquid tornado it seemed to burp us back to the surface. Suddenly the furious current seemed to let us go, and I was finally able to push us toward the edge of the water. I began to feel the muddy bottom of the ditch, which pulled on my feet with each step. When we gained enough footing to stand, I told her to give me the baby, which I pulled over her shoulder.

I tried not to panic when I saw the wide-eyed daze on the baby's face, and I couldn't tell whether it was breathing. I pulled the infant's stomach against my shoulder and began to firmly thump its back, hoping that if it had swallowed water that this would make it regurgitate. I could hear the mother praying for her child as we struggled through the mud. After about a half dozen thumps, with no apparent response, I began to get desperate, so I gave the baby a much harder thump than I wanted to. When I did, I heard a sputter, then some coughs, and finally the baby began to scream at the top of its lungs. I never could have imagined that sound being so welcome. I could hear the mother breathlessly thanking God, as we stepped out of the water. I could see that the woman was limping badly, so I came along side of her and helped her walk up the slope from the ditch. We'd only taken a few steps from the water when we were met by a police officer, a couple of paramedics and a host of apparently concerned onlookers. As the paramedics began working on the woman and her baby, the officer asked me how I was doing. I told him that I just needed to sit down, but as he was helping me to the ground I apparently passed out.

When I regained consciousness, I was in a private hospital room with Claire sitting by my bed, watching television. She seemed genuinely relieved that I was awake, and that other than a pretty bad headache, I felt alright. She summoned the doctor, who asked me a few questions before explaining that my body had most likely gone into a state of shock in response to the trauma of the situation. He explained that they wanted to keep me in the hospital overnight for observation. After he left, Claire began to fill me in on all the details I had missed, like the name of the woman and her baby, their condition, the status of my wrecked car, and the ticket that I received for the accident. She also let me know that someone who had been at the intersection had recorded the entire ordeal on their cell phone, and that it had already been aired on the evening news. Later that night as I watched the clip, it seemed more like a dream than reality. The clip ended with a shot of me helping the lady out of the water with one hand and holding the baby in the other; and for the first time I recognized that Billy Turner's vision had come to pass.

"Oh, my God!" I gasped.

"What's wrong, Honey?" Claire asked.

"Oh, my God!" I repeated.

"Honey, what is wrong?"

"Billy Turner's vision!" I exclaimed.

"What?"

"Billy Turner told me he had a vision of me helping some dark haired lady in a river and holding a baby," I said in amazement.

"What?"

"I'm telling you, that kid described this scene to me two days ago in my office."

"That's ridiculous, Bob! It must be some sort of coincidence," she chided.

"Come on, Claire, even you would have to admit that this is a pretty incredible coincidence."

"So, what are you saying, Bob? Are you now ready to claim that God is telling some little kid the future?"

I unconsciously retreated by saying, "No, I'm not claiming anything. I mean, I'm just saying that this is exactly what the kid described to me."

"Look, Bob, I know that you've been under a lot stress with this and that you really want to help this kid. But you'd better be careful or you're in real danger of getting pulled into some religious fantasy. If that happens, you can probably kiss your career in public education goodbye. Now you've had a rough day, so maybe what you need to do is rest," she said in mock consolation.

I hated being patronized, but I knew that it was useless trying to talk about something like this with Claire, so I closed my eyes and let her believe that I was resting. Within a couple of minutes she turned off the television and headed home. Like me, Claire had been raised in church, and though she never really explained, I got the feeling that her experience had been damaging. While I was simply ambivalent about religion, she was clearly bitter towards it.

I certainly wasn't comfortable with the idea that God may have shown Billy the future, but I couldn't just dismiss it as a coincidence either. If it really was from God, what was He trying to tell me? I remembered what Mrs. Turner had said about His voice, and I once again began searching my thoughts for something that might have been from Him. Within a couple of minutes, a nurse came in to check my vitals, and when I looked up I was shocked to see that it was Mrs. Turner. She was as surprised to see me as I was to see her. I found out that she normally didn't work the graveyard shift, but that she was making up the time that she'd missed for our meeting. I told her the story of how I wound up in the hospital, and she mentioned that she'd seen the clip on television, but hadn't realized it was me. I again found myself full of burning questions, so I decided to share Billy's vision with her.

"Do you remember the end of the clip that they showed on the news, where I'm helping the lady out of the water and holding the baby?"

"Yes."

"Billy described that scene to me in my office the other day. He said that God had showed it to him in a vision."

"Well, that is one of the ways that Billy hears and sees things," she confirmed.

"Have you ever had a vision, Mrs. Turner?"

"Yes, Mr. Davis, I have, and my patients normally just call me Susan."

"Why would God show Billy something like that?" I queried.

"I'd guess that He was trying to show you what is truth and what is not," she replied.

"Do you think it means that He wants me to defend Billy?"

"Maybe, but I suspect this isn't as much about Billy as it is about you."

"What about me?"

"I don't know," she admitted.

"Please, I need your help. If God is trying to say something to me, then I don't want to miss it," I pleaded.

"You can be sure that God is trying to say something to you," she said with an eerie confidence.

"But what?" I asked.

"I don't know, but like I told you before, if you belong to Him then you have the ability to hear Him."

"What if I don't?" I asked pensively.

"What if you don't … what?" she inquired.

As our eyes met, I said, "What if I don't belong to Him?"

"Do you doubt that you belong to Him?" she asked gently.

"I didn't, but now I'm not so sure. I was raised to believe that all you needed to do was to believe in Him and to try to be a good person. Is that wrong?"

"Well, maybe not wrong, but at least a little incomplete. We do need to believe, but that belief has to penetrate our hearts. If that happens, it changes the way that we live, and as we walk in relationship with Him, we begin to reflect His character. It is not our righteousness that matters; it is taking on His righteousness," she explained.

"I've always believed that He's up there, but I guess I'm not sure how to have a relationship with a God that I cannot see."

"The Bible says, 'Behold, I stand at the door and knock; if anyone hears My voice, and opens the door, I will come in and dine with them.' I believe that what you've been experiencing these last couple of days is God knocking on the door of your heart. I believe that if you'll invite Him, He'll come into your heart, and that you can begin to have this relationship that He desires," she said.

"You make it sound very simple."

"It is very simple, but it's not always easy."

"What do you mean?" I asked.

"God will do His part, but our human nature tends to fight God's plan for us. The decision to live for Him means that you will have to forfeit your plan for your life."

In a tone befitting my sense of brokenness, I admitted, "I'm not really sure what my plan is. For that matter I'm not even sure that I have a plan at all."

"Believe me, His plans are much better than anything that we could come up with, but to really live for Him will cost you everything," she said.

"These last couple of days have really made me wonder what I believe and maybe even what I really want."

"Only God can show you the truth of your heart."

"I want that," I said.

"Then let's invite Him in," she offered.

Mrs. Turner took my hand and led me through a simple prayer of invitation and surrender. Though she had to get back to her duties, she told me to close my eyes and to picture opening a door within myself. Though I was not normally a very visual person, this turned out to be much easier than I imagined. As I did, waves of peace seemed to wash over me and it felt as though heavy, wet, sand bags had been lifted from my shoulders. It seemed as though I was weightless, and that I might even float off the bed. Grateful tears began to well up in my eyes and stream down my face. I hadn't cried in years, and once I started, it seemed that I might not be able to stop. It occurred to me that the overwhelming sense of loneliness that had haunted me since my childhood had somehow departed as well, and I felt as though God had drawn near to me. Again, I found myself feeling like a little boy, one who'd taken a hot bath and was now in a warm, safe place. After what seemed like a long time, I drifted off into a deep and restful sleep.

While I felt as though I'd slept through the night, it was only a couple of hours later when Mrs. Turner returned to again check my vitals. I was excited to talk to her about what I was feeling, and she seemed to know a scripture that validated everything I was sensing. After several minutes of discussing what was going on inside of me, my thoughts turned back to the situation with Billy and Jared.

"Mrs. Turner, can I ask you a question that's been bothering me since we talked in my office?"

"Certainly, Mr. Davis."

"If you felt like it was totally inappropriate for someone Billy's age to be trying to cast demons out of people, then why teach him how to do it?"

"I didn't intentionally teach him to do that," she replied.

"I guess I don't understand how that could come across by accident?" I said.

"The difficult thing about Billy's gift is that he is sensitive to spiritual things, which not only encompasses the things of heaven, but also the powers of darkness. When Billy interacts with the light, he can seem older, stronger and wiser than a little boy could ever be, but at his young age, the powers of darkness can grab a hold of him and make him almost unrecognizable as the kindhearted little boy that he really is. I've tried to teach him how to discern the different forces that are at work in him at any given moment and how to deal with the forces of darkness. I felt like it was necessary for his survival, and I believe that he does a pretty good job of recognizing and fighting off the demonic. What I didn't anticipate was that he'd begin to discern these things in other people and decide to fight for them, too."

"It's amazing to hear you talk about this, it sounds as though the battle never ends."

"It doesn't, but it's really no different for you and me. There are forces working on us all the time, we just aren't as aware of what is powering them, as Billy is. The Bible teaches that what is seen is temporary, but what is unseen is eternal. Most people live their lives as though what is seen is reality and what is unseen is imaginary," she explained.

"It's kind of scary to think that there are forces working against me that I can't see."

"As children of God, we are protected by the blood of Jesus. While that doesn't mean that demons can't attack us, it does mean that we have the authority to cast them down in Jesus' name. What is scary is someone like the little boy that Billy prayed for."

"You mean Jared?" I asked.

"Yes, a boy like that is likely to be unprotected against such things," she replied.

This confused me, as I asked, "But I thought that Billy was successful in making the demon go away?"

"Even if he was, the doorway through which that demon entered is likely to remain open and so it is likely to return."

"What do you mean when you talk about a doorway?" I inquired.

"I suspect that there are things going on in that boy's life that give the powers of darkness access to and authority within him. Without the power of God, he is unlikely to understand those forces or to successfully fight them off," she said sadly.

"Would something like abuse cause that?" I asked.

"Absolutely," she replied.

"What can we do?"

"We can pray for that little boy and do our best to dispatch the resources of heaven on his behalf."

"And what should I do about Billy?" I continued.

"As I mentioned before, Billy is in God's hands. You do whatever you feel the Lord is telling you to do. If He's called you, He'll equip you. But if He's not calling you to a battle, don't try to fight one," she warned.

"I guess that I'm a little afraid that I won't be able to hear Him," I confessed.

"Well let's pray that God will show us both the way to go."

Mrs. Turner once again took my hands and quietly began to pray. She asked God to guide us, praying that we wouldn't struggle with which way to turn. That He would open and close doors for us, and that He would give us peace in our journey. Her hands began to tremble and she began to pray in a mumble beneath her breath. I could feel a tingling sensation run from my hands, up my arms and neck, to the top of my head. It was a strangely exhilarating feeling and I sensed that it might be from God. Tears once again began to well up at the thought of God's nearness and of His concern.

With my eyes closed, I began to see a picture in my mind. It was Principle Skinner, sitting in a big, high backed, chair, and I was sitting right next to him on a little stool. I seemed very small, and as I looked closer, I saw that my hands, feet and mouth were wrapped in silver duct tape. Nothing was happening, it was just a picture. I heard Mrs. Turner say, "Amen," and I felt her let go of my hands. I thanked her for all that she'd done and she reassured me that everything was going to be OK. I found myself ready to sleep again, and as I laid my head back I could still feel the tingling in my arms and neck. As I closed my eyes, I felt that same wave of peace roll over me, and I was asleep almost instantly.

V. A Change of Mind

I slept for several hours after that, missing breakfast and lunch in the process. When the doctor came in the afternoon he decided to send me home, though, to my surprise he ordered at least two days of complete bed rest. This seemed to annoy Claire for some reason, but I welcomed the break. I continued to feel the effects of the prayer that I'd prayed with Mrs. Turner, all tingly and childlike on the inside. Several of the Bible passages that she had quoted kept running through my mind, and even though I had heard most of them before, they seemed to be impacting me in a way that they never had. I yearned to talk about it, but I knew not to say a word to Claire. I remembered that there was a Bible somewhere in my pile of books, and for the first time I found myself wanting to read it. While I was lost in my thoughts, I kept catching Claire looking at me as if I'd grown a second head. I asked her about it, but she denied anything was wrong. She claimed to be worried about me, but I could tell that wasn't it. Since she wasn't willing to talk about it, I decided to let it go, and my thoughts drifted back toward spiritual things.

When we got home, I immediately headed to my bookshelf; sure that I'd find the Bible grouped with the classics. I guess that's how I'd viewed it up to that point, a piece of classic literature that I wasn't very interested in reading. Now, like a sudden urge for Shakespeare, I wanted not only to read it, but to understand it. Sure enough, I found it right between "A Tale of Two Cities" and "For Whom the Bell Tolls." As I walked toward the bedroom, I caught Claire glaring at me again, but I again chose to ignore her. I set the book on my nightstand as I changed my clothes, intending to read some before I slept.

But a sudden wave of tiredness swept over me as I sat down and so I decided to sleep first. As I laid my head on the pillow, I thought of Claire and how unhappy she seemed to be. Without thinking I said, "Lord, help her." I pictured her frowning face, and my heart felt heavy, as I once again drifted into a deep sleep.

After all the sleep I'd gotten in the hospital, I expected just to nap for an hour or two and then maybe have some dinner with Claire. But when I awoke, I rolled over to see that I'd slept through the night, and that it was already after eight the next morning. I wondered why Claire hadn't awakened me, and it suddenly dawned on me that I'd never called Principal Skinner to let him know what the doctor had ordered. I rolled across the bed, grabbed the phone, and quickly dialed the school's office. The secretary put me right through, and I caught myself being somewhat surprised by Mike Skinner's friendly, upbeat manner.

"Bob! It's so good to hear your voice."

"Well, thanks, uh Mike."

"So, Claire tells me that you're really exhausted," he said.

"You spoke with Claire?" I gasped.

"Yes, she called me last night to let me know what was happening. She said you were asleep."

"Uh, yeah, I have been sleeping a lot since the accident," I stammered.

"Well, Bob, we want you to get all the rest that you need. I don't want you to worry about things here, we've got it covered."

"I appreciate your concern Mike, but I know that we've got to get moving on this Billy Turner issue," I began.

Cutting me off before I could finish, he said, "Bob, please don't concern yourself about the Billy Turner thing. There are more important things in life than work, and I can mind the shop while you're away. You just need to focus on getting rest and feeling better. I don't want you to come back until you're feeling 100%."

"Well, that's very generous Mike, but maybe we ought to discuss some other things that I've run into during my investigation."

"No, Bob, I don't want you to even think about this. I just want you to focus on getting better. I've got your notes and if I need anything else, I can always call. Like I told Claire last night, you just need to take a little break from all this," he said in what seemed to be a patronizing voice.

"Again, Mike, I appreciate your concern but," I started.

"No buts, Bob, rest!" he interrupted.

"Well I."

"No more, Bob, rest!"

"OK, rest," I said weakly.

"Good, well, now that we've settled that, I've got some people waiting to talk to me, so I really need to go."

It struck me that Mike's pleasant demeanor had substantially evaporated over the course of our short conversation, and I got the distinct impression that he really didn't want to talk to me. It was odd that Claire had called him at home. That was not like her at all, and I wondered how he had my notes when they'd been locked in my desk. While it was not unreasonable for a principal to have that kind of control within a school, I got the sense that there was something going on, and that Mike Skinner was pleased to have me out of the picture. I remembered the picture that I'd seen in my mind earlier with duct tape over my mouth, and I felt a wave of anxiety wash over me. I felt almost desperate to get to the school, but how could I explain my reason for ignoring the doctor's orders? I wondered what Claire said to Mike, and that same ominous feeling began to rise up in me. I thought about calling Mrs. Turner, but when I pictured her face, I knew that she'd just tell me to calm down and to pray for direction.

Even though I still had no confidence that I'd hear anything, I decided to try to pray. As I lay across the bed, I started to speak in the formal way that I'd heard people pray in church as a child, but it seemed so phony that I had to stop. I closed my eyes and again pictured a door opening within me; I simply said, "Please help me Lord," and a warm tingling sensation began to slowly roll from the top of my head to the tips of my feet. It was as though someone had poured warm syrup on my head, and it slowly worked its way completely across my body. That tremendous sense of peace that was beginning to become familiar to me accompanied these physical sensations and the scripture that talks about a peace that surpasses understanding flashed through my mind.

I reached for my bedside table wondering if I could find that passage in the Bible, but, to my surprise, it wasn't there. While I'd been a little fuzzy about some of the details in the last couple of days, I was absolutely clear that I'd left the Bible on the bedside table. I looked around the bedroom some and then wandered back into the living room, where I found it back on the bookshelf. The thought that Claire had moved it irritated me, and that agitation began to push away the peace that had accompanied my prayer. I closed my eyes and took a deep breath and I could almost sense the forces of darkness pushing against me. I felt like my heart was pounding in my chest and I started to feel a little light headed. I wanted to go lie back down, but I decided to grab the Bible and committed to reading something before I took another nap.

I sat on the couch hoping to find the passage about peace, and with some help from the index, I was soon reading in the book of Philippians. It said that I shouldn't be anxious for anything and that I just needed to make my requests known to God. Something about these words resonated in me and I again felt like a little child. I set the Bible back on my bookshelf and went back to the bedroom. As I lay across the bed I once again began to pray in a very childlike manner, asking God to help me to understand what was happening and what I should do. Tears began to stream from my eyes and within a few minutes, I was sobbing uncontrollably. I really had no idea why, but I felt as though all of this emotion had been bottled up within me for years, and that there was something cleansing about releasing it.

It seemed to come in waves, with all sorts of images running through my mind. I saw the woman dragged from the bed of adultery; I saw Jesus being baptized; I saw myself as a child. I saw my father; I saw Jesus on the cross; I saw a cat that I had when I was young. I saw Billy Turner; I saw myself stepping out of a boat onto rolling water; I saw Claire's angry face. I saw myself weeping at Jesus' bloody feet. Every image brought a sense of profound purpose, though I couldn't seem to grasp what it all meant. Despite my lack of understanding, each one seemed to spark another wave of emotion. I felt like a bottle of soda that had been violently shaken and then opened. It was exhilarating and almost painful and ultimately exhausting. After what seemed to be hours, the waves subsided and I once again fell into a deep sleep.

The next couple of days were a blur. I'd sleep for a couple of hours and then read the Bible for hours. I'd always thought of the Bible as an ancient book about ancient times, but as I read it seemed as though every word was applicable to my life. Claire became invisible, getting up early, coming home late, and avoiding every attempt at conversation with the line, "You need your rest". I felt totally disconnected from the world, and that seemed to make God and the things the Bible said seem more real to me. I caught myself casually speaking to God about what I was reading, and I genuinely sensed that He was listening. I had no desire to return to my old life, but every time I saw Claire, I knew that there was no way to avoid it. The more I was moved by my revelation of God, the deeper the hole was getting for Claire and me.

I understood that not only was Claire not willing to take this journey, she wasn't willing to tolerate my taking it either. As I read the scriptures I realized that we were "unequally yoked," not in step with each other, not headed in the same direction, and not trying to get to the same destination. It hurt to think about it, so I'd just push it away and read some more. I was so immersed in my own thoughts and life that for those few days I actually forgot about the situation at school, but on the evening of the third day I remembered, and I knew it was time to go back. I decided not to call and let them know I was coming back, so that if there really was something going on behind my back, I might walk in on it.

VI. Blindside

All the way into work the next morning I tried to come up with the words that I'd use to explain to Mike that Billy was legitimate and posed no real threat to the other kids, but everything I came up with sounded ludicrous. Mike had a ferocious gift for cross-examination and I could imagine him ripping apart every word I said. I remembered what Mrs. Turner had said about spiritual things being spiritually discerned, and I began to feel the pressure building inside of me. All I could think to do was pray, "I must decrease, and You must increase," over and over again. While I never reached a place of peace, it did seem to keep the pressure from building any further.

I arrived at the school not knowing what was going to happen or what I was going to say. I decided just to let the secretary know that I was back, in hopes of avoiding an immediate conversation with Mike, but, to my surprise, she told me that Mike had been expecting me and that he'd left a message for me to meet him at the district administration building by 8:30 a.m. As I walked back out to my car, I was baffled at how Mike could have known that I'd be coming back on that morning when I didn't even know myself until the night before, but then it hit me like lightning, "Claire had called him!" The thought made me furious and more convinced than ever that something was going on. I caught myself wanting to go to her office and to cause a big scene, but I knew that there was no time for that. My mind spun with the possible scenarios that I might be walking into. I was fairly certain that this couldn't be the official hearing before the district advisory board. After all, there hadn't been enough time to set that up, and Mike wouldn't want me to walk into that unprepared, because that could reflect poorly on him.

But, if that wasn't what was happening, why were we meeting at the district's building and not at the school? I was sweating by the time I pulled into the parking lot, and a quick check of the clock in my car let me know that I only had about five minutes to spare. I resisted the urge to run across the parking lot, though I'm sure I looked pretty ridiculous as I race-walked toward the building. I could feel the sweat running down my temples as I asked the receptionist where I could find Principal Skinner, and my heart began to pound when she pointed me to the advisory board's hearing room.

As I came through the door I was surprised by how crowded the room was, and I saw Mike nearly hurdle his chair to get to me. He had a big smile on his face, but I could tell that he wasn't pleased to see me.

"Bob, it is so good to see you back on your feet again. I see you got my message."

"Yes, but not until I got to the school!" I replied in a tone that conveyed my irritation.

"Well, yes, everything has been very rushed, but I'm glad you're here."

"Mike, what's going on?" I said.

"Well, Bob, there really isn't time to explain, the Board is ready to start," he replied.

"But, Mike, are you expecting me to be a part of this? I've not had a chance to prepare anything."

"Don't worry, Bob, your part will be very simple. Just sit at the table with me, and we'll get started."

I felt sick to my stomach as I followed Mike back to the front of the room. I saw Mr. And Mrs. Lowe sitting on either side of Jared and eyeing everyone warily. I tried to make eye contact with Jared, but he stared straight ahead like a zombie; he looked miserable. On the other side of the room I saw Billy and Mrs. Turner. When our eyes met Mrs. Turner smiled. And when Billy saw me, he jumped up from his chair and ran to me. He reached his hand out and in an inappropriately loud voice said, "Hi, Mr. Davis!" I tried to respond in a much quieter voice, hoping to avoid any more attention.

"Hi, Billy, how are you doing?"

"OK, I guess. Am I in big trouble?"

"You're not in big trouble with me," I replied.

"That's good, but what about those guys over there?" he said as he pointed toward the board members.

"You know, Billy, I'm not really sure about them"

"Are you in trouble with those guys?" he asked innocently.

"You know, I'm not sure about that either," I admitted.

"Oh, well, I guess we're just gonna have to pray huh?" he concluded in typical Billy fashion.

"Yes, Billy, I think we better."

"I heard about your accident. Are you OK?"

"Yes, I'm doing much better."

"Yea, I saw it on the TV. It was just like that vision, huh?"

I realized that this conversation had the potential to make things worse for Billy, and I could see that they were ready to start, so I told him that he should probably go sit down. I found myself having strong paternal feelings for this little boy, which was very unusual for me. I had always maintained a certain detachment from the kids, so that my position would never be compromised. While I'd never worked up the nerve to ask about Mr. Turner, I found myself irritated that he wasn't there to fight for his son. Billy was a precious kid, and I was ready to fight for him. As I looked back to the Lowe's, I felt a wave of disgust roll over me. I hated what they were putting the Turner's through, and I hated what I imagined they were doing to their son.

As I stared at Jared, I began to sense a vague shadow behind him. At first I thought that it must be something strange with the lighting, but soon the image grew more distinct. I was aware that I was staring, but I couldn't seem to take my eyes off of him. The shadow seemed to be like a tall being, standing directly behind him and leaning over him in an imposing way. As the image of its arms became clearer, I could see that it was powerfully built and that its skin was covered in what looked to be scales. As my eyes studied this image, I realized that this thing had its hands tightly wrapped around Jared's throat. A wave of panic began to rise in me and my arms and legs seemed to go limp. I instinctively opened my mouth to say something, but it was as if every bit of moisture in my mouth were gone. Suddenly this thing turned its ugly head toward me, its face seemingly a cross between a wolf and an alligator. It looked me right in the eye and began to laugh mockingly.

I let out an audible gasp, and my trance-like state was shattered by the sound of Principal Skinner's whispering voice. He asked if I was OK, and I nodded at him, as I tried to regain my composure. When I glanced back at Jared, the image was gone and I wondered if I'd just had a vision. As I pondered what it might mean, it occurred to me that the Lowe's weren't sitting on either side of Jared to protect him, but that they were really guarding him for that thing. I felt like I was going to be sick, and I had to turn my face and my thoughts away from them.

Turning my attention back to the hearing, I noticed a man sitting on the other side of Mike Skinner, with his chair close enough to the table to give the appearance that he was sitting with us. While I knew almost everyone in the room, this man didn't look familiar to me. I didn't think much of it at the time, and I only half-listened as the advisory board chairman explained the rules for the hearing. He explained that, while this was not a court of law, transcripts from this proceeding would be admissible in court, and that the hearing would be handled in much the same manner. Principal Skinner was to be the lone voice representing the school, unless he or the board felt the need to call witnesses.

It all seemed fairly standard, as Mike began to explain how he'd first heard of the incident, and the immediate steps he'd taken. It was generally understood that even though this wasn't a real court, having the children testify was something to be avoided. So it was a great surprise when he called on Billy to speak. I had the urge to jump up and shout "Objection!" but I resisted it. Mike smiled at Billy and talked in an overly friendly way, giving him some patronizing instructions about telling the truth and only answering the questions that were asked. In typical Billy-fashion, he simply chirped, "OK." Mike asked him to give his account of what had happened on the playground that day, and Billy gladly complied. He held back nothing and showed no signs of remorse as he recollected.

Periodically, Mike would repeat little phrases and words for emphasis, like, "So, you actually saw the demon" or, "So, God told you." I had to love Billy's honest heart, but having him tell this story couldn't have been more damaging. I consoled myself with what Mrs. Turner had said about there being no disagreement about what had happened, but that, ultimately, the disagreement was about what it meant. While having Billy tell the story made it seem more sensational, hopefully I would be able to steer the panel back some with my explanation of what it all meant. It occurred to me that I should probably mention Billy's constitutional rights to express his religious beliefs, to give the board something to think about. I glanced back at Mrs. Turner, but her eyes were fixed on Billy, and I was pretty sure that she was praying under her breath. When Billy was dismissed from questioning I tried to convince myself that the worst was over and that we'd just need to work on a recovery. Unfortunately, I was wrong.

In yet another surprising move, Principal Skinner then called Mrs. Phillips for questioning. This broke another unspoken rule about teachers testifying in front of their students, and it seemed totally unnecessary to me. After all, there was no disagreement about what happened, and Mrs. Phillips was an emotional wreck under the best of circumstances. Her testimony somehow managed to be even more sensational than Billy's account, as Mike kept asking her how she felt during this episode. She cried and talked about how traumatizing it was and how afraid she was that Billy might hurt her or Jared. It was a circus, and Mike Skinner seemed to be the ring master. Why should the board care about how Mrs Phillips was feeling, and what exactly was a kid as small as Billy Turner going to do to hurt either her or Jared? I remember thinking that if she was that terrified of an eight year old she ought to think of a career change.

Blessedly, they let her go back to her seat, and I hoped we were now finally done with this phase of the testimony, but then Mike called Mr. Lowe to testify. I was furious. What could this man possibly say? He wasn't even there. Why would the board need to listen to this guy, and what did Principal Skinner hope to accomplish with this? I could feel my face twisting with disgust as Mike explained that while he wanted to present Jared's side of the story, poor Jared was just too traumatized to speak for himself. Of course, Mr. Lowe had graciously stepped up to speak for him, but Mike never really asked him about the particulars of what happened. Instead he asked, "How has all of this affected your family?" This opened the door for Mr. Lowe to go on a twenty minute rant on how damaging this had been, not only to Jared, but to the whole family. I fumed as I listened to him blame this incident for just about every problem that they had as a family, including his not having a job. I couldn't wait to get up there and tell the board about what Jared had told me and of my suspicions about the Lowes. I might be committing professional suicide, but there was no way I was going to play along with this charade. A picture of Claire flashed in my mind, and I realized how angry she would be with me. But I didn't care. I had to do the right thing, no matter what it cost.

Finally, Mike called my name, and I made my way to the podium. My hands shook as I braced myself for what was sure to be a contentious exchange. There was no way that I was going to let Mike twist my words or sensationalize what I saw and heard. He explained to the board about my accident and let them know that this was my first day back. I assumed this was his way of covering himself in case I really blew it. After these preliminaries, he turned to me.

"Mr. Davis, did you have the opportunity to interview Billy Turner after this incident?"

"Yes sir, I did."

Mike handed me a copy of my notes from my interview with Billy.

"And are these the notes that you took in conjunction with that interview?"

"Yes sir, they are."

"Mr. Davis, are you a licensed psychologist?"

"No sir, I am not."

"Thank you, Mr. Davis, you may be seated."

"Excuse me?"

"You may sit down, Mr. Davis."

I was so caught off guard that I simply stared at Him. I wanted to say something, but my mind went completely blank. What in God's name was he doing? I again remembered the picture of me sitting on the little stool with duct tape over my mouth and I felt as though I was underwater as I shuffled back to the table, wondering where he was going to go from here. That's when he called, "Dr. Brandon Smith" to the podium. I had never heard the name, and, sure enough, the mystery man sitting on the other end of the table stood up. I could feel my anger rising as Mike explained to the board that Dr. Smith was a licensed psychologist, who had been brought in to assess the data that I had collected. Of course, the only data that was in writing was what was gathered during Billy's interview, as I'd never gotten the chance to document my discussion with Jared.

Principal Skinner then requested that Billy and Jared be removed from the hearing room due to the "sensitive nature" of what Dr. Smith had to say. Even though I agreed with this action in principle, it irritated me that, after ignoring all of the other sensitivity issues, he was going to make a big show of this one. My heart broke for Mrs. Turner as I watched her escort Billy out of the room, and my anger with Mike began to give way to discouragement. I wondered why God wasn't doing something about all of this. After all, these were His kids, and they really believed in Him.

Dr. Smith wasted no time in painting a vivid picture for the board. He was given free reign to discuss a whole range of psychological issues (e.g. Attention Deficit Disorder, schizophrenia, paranoid delusion...), all of which, presumably, applied to Billy in some way. He even drew a parallel between Billy and the childhood psychological profiles of famous serial killers. Unfortunately, he kept referring to things that I'd written in my notes, giving the impression that we could be in total agreement in regard to his conclusions. Even after he'd made his position clear, Mike kept asking leading questions, seemingly in an effort to pound the point home for the committee. When he asked Dr. Smith's "professional opinion" on whether Billy presented any real threat to the other kids, he, once again, quoted my notes for his reply; "I think that Mr. Davis makes an excellent point in his notes when he mentions that it is not only the fact that Billy hears voices, but that he's willing to act on what they tell him." With that as his basis, Dr. Smith went on to explain that he didn't feel as though Billy should be allowed to return to a regular classroom setting.

Once again, I felt nauseous as they used my words to finish Billy off. Mike Skinner had not only managed to crucify this little boy, but he'd used nails that I'd given him, and the hammer of Dr. Smith's supposed expertise, to do it. In his closing remarks he took on the role of Pontius Pilate, saying "Based on the findings of Mr. Davis' investigation and Dr. Smith's expert assessment, I have no choice but to recommend that Billy Turner be removed from regular classes, on a permanent basis." I sat in stunned silence, as I realized that Mike had successfully presented this case as nothing more than a documentary, when, in truth, it had been a purely theatrical production. One that he'd written, directed, and in which he was the lead actor. While I couldn't bear to look him in the eye, and though I would never trust him again, it was impossible to deny the man's genius.

I slumped in my chair with my eyes fixed on the floor as I listened to the board unanimously accept the school's recommendations. I was almost afraid to make eye contact with anyone, unsure of whether I might scream or burst into tears. The chairman went on to explain that Billy's case would now be deferred to the state school board, who would assess him for placement in a state run program created for children with "special needs." I seethed at the thought that they'd successfully hung a label on this child--a label that would likely follow him for the rest of his life. I found myself searching for words of consolation for Billy and Mrs. Turner, but I couldn't seem to come up with any. I didn't suppose that it would matter much, as they probably wouldn't want to speak to me after Mike's little show before the board. I could feel a knot the size of a fist in my stomach, and I could no longer contain my grief, as tears began to seep from my eyes. I put my head in my hands, hoping that no one would see that I was crying. It took all of my strength not to break into a sob. I kept seeing Billy's face in my mind, and his eyes seemed to be asking me to explain what had just happened. All I could think to say was, "I'm so sorry."

After several minutes in a fog of thoughts, I realized that the room had grown quiet, and as I pulled my head from my hands, it began to throb. Thinking I was alone, I slowly got up and turned to leave. But as I raised my eyes I saw Billy and Mrs. Turner sitting silently in the back of the room. The sight of them was more than I could take, and I burst into tears. Billy jumped to his feet and ran to me, throwing his arms around me and burying his face in my chest. My body began to shake, as waves of shame and embarrassment at my failure mixed with love and fear for Billy. I'd never had such strong feelings for anyone or anything before, and I wondered if this is what it felt like to be a parent. I was overwhelmed. Mrs. Turner made her way to me and put her hand on my shoulder, squeezing it slightly. She quietly said, "It's going to be alright." I didn't understand how she could say that, and, for a moment, I wondered if she understood what they'd just decided. But as our eyes met, I somehow knew that she did, and that she had already managed to get beyond it. I found myself being amazed by her faith, and wondering what it would take for me to get to that place. Billy's cheerful voice interrupted that thought, as he said:

"Don't worry, Mr. Davis, I'm gonna be OK," he said confidently.

"I hope so, Billy," I gasped.

"Yep, momma says that God's got a plan for me and that it really didn't matter what happened today.'"

"Well, you keep listening to your momma, Billy, she's a very smart lady," I replied.

"I know!"

As I turned my attention to Mrs. Turner, she said, "It really is going to be fine."

"But what are you going to do?" I asked.

"I don't really know yet, but the Lord showed me that this was coming, so I'm sure He'll guide us through it."

I could barely conceal my shame as I said, "I'm so sorry that I wasn't more of a help to you."

"Don't be silly, you did everything that you could," she replied.

"Which, in this case, turned out to be just about nothing," I moaned.

"Mr Davis, this was out of your hands from the beginning. Don't take responsibility for something that was never yours to fix."

"I just hate the way it turned out," I replied.

"Well, the Lord promises that He'll work all things to the good of those who love Him and who are called to His purpose."

"Well, this certainly didn't work out well," I said bitterly.

"It's not over yet. Life is a journey, and we'll need to get down the road some before we'll really understand what all of this meant."

As with everything that Mrs. Turner said, I sensed incredible faith, wisdom, and patience in her words, though I have to admit that a very quiet voice in the back of my mind always wondered if she wasn't just kidding herself. I hugged them both and thanked them for everything that they'd done for me. I walked them out to the parking lot and waved as they drove away. I don't know why, but I somehow imagined that we would stay in touch, but that didn't happen. After a few years I assumed that I'd never see either of them again, and, until I turned on the television this morning, that had been true.

VII. Call the Doctor!

While my eyes had continued to be locked on the television screen, my mind had been completely consumed with memories. By the time I was ready to step back into the present, the program segment was ending. While Billy appeared to be testifying before some type of committee, it wasn't clear to me what it was about. Right before the camera came off of him, they flashed a caption at the bottom of the screen which said, "Dr. William Turner – Arizona State University." It was all I could do not to scream; "Dr. William Turner!" "Dr. William Turner!" "Praise God!" I couldn't believe it. Here I'd thought that this boy's life had been destroyed, and, instead, I find out that he is "Dr. William Turner." Grateful tears began to flow as I considered the sovereignty of God. Mrs. Turner had been right. God had a plan for Billy, and no man was able to steal that from him.

This made me think about my own life and how it had changed in the last twenty five years. I marveled at how God had managed to take that difficult situation and work it to my good. After Billy's hearing I promised myself that I would not continue to work for Mike Skinner, and I immediately began working on my resume. But before I was able to send out the first one, Mike was promoted to a special advisor position for the school district. The local press had really grabbed a hold of Billy's story, making Mike out to be some sort of civil rights crusader. Soon after that, the national press snatched up the story, too. Within six months of his promotion to the district job Mike was lured away by a big school district in the San Francisco area. Years later he became the president of the National Education Association (NEA), which is a powerful Washington based lobby group that seeks to influence the government's policies on education. I couldn't help but think that Washington was the perfect place for a guy like Mike.

Though his departure ultimately saved my job, there wasn't anything that could save my marriage. Claire and I emerged from this incident on totally separate paths and by the end of the school year I discovered that she was having an affair with one of her clients. We were divorced a few months later, and soon after her boyfriend's divorce, they were married.

Though the divorce had been painful, it is hard to imagine what my life would have been like without it. Becoming single again allowed me to take a hard look at what I really wanted out of life and to explore my faith in a way that I never could have with Claire. Though I often felt lonely in that season, I decided not to pursue another relationship, and it was during that period that God became real to me. I decided to just try to live for Him and not worry about myself, which was somehow incredibly liberating. The less I worried about temporal things, the more God seemed to intervene on my behalf.

A couple of years after that I met a wonderful woman named Katherine at church. Like me, she was a school teacher and wasn't actively pursuing a relationship with anyone. Her husband had been killed in a car accident, and she was raising their two young children by herself. Our friendship eventually blossomed into courtship and ultimately led to our marriage. We have now been married for over twenty years, and it has made all the difference in my life. Her love for me has been such a blessing. Her love of God has strengthened my walk of faith, and her children have become our children. Somehow God used all of these things to bring me closer to Him and to restore my hope for the future.

In the excitement of the moment, I decided to search the web for information about "Dr. William Turner," but, to my surprise,

I got over two million hits on that name. So I decided to check on the website for Arizona State University. Sure enough, Dr. Billy's bio was included on the "Faculty" page. I couldn't believe my eyes as I read of his achievements; a Bachelors degree in Education (earned at the age of 19); a Master's degree in Early Childhood Development (earned at age 22); completed his doctorate by the age of 25; awarded a research grant at Stanford University to study the long-term effects of medication on children diagnosed with Attention Deficit Disorders. Co-authored multiple texts pertaining to innovation and reform within the traditional education model; appointed to the President's Council on Education Reform; appointed to the President's Council on Faith Based Initiatives; full professor in the Education Department at Arizona State University, and numerous other awards and accolades. It was hard to believe that someone in his early thirties could have accomplished so much.

All of this just whetted my appetite to know more. I knew that Tempe, Arizona was only about a six-hour drive from where I lived, and I decided that I had to go see Billy. I could barely contain my excitement as I waited for Katherine to get back from her morning walk, and I nearly knocked her over as she came through the door. She listened patiently as I went on and on about what I'd discovered and explained that I had to go see Billy right away. She seemed to understand my need to go, but calmly suggested that we call the university to try to make an appointment before we embarked on such a road trip. Of course, she was right, and after working my way through multiple automated operators, I finally got a hold of the secretary who maintained his calendar. She agreed to schedule me for an appointment with him on the following Friday, at 10:00 a.m. Even though that was only a couple of days away, the wait was excruciating. Early Thursday afternoon, Katherine and I were on our way to Tempe.

While Katherine had heard most of the Billy Turner story before, I kept recalling little details that I hadn't thought of in years. I'm sure that she was getting a little tired of hearing about it; but ,as always, she listened patiently. That night in the hotel she asked if I thought that Billy would remember me. And for the first time I recognized the reasonable potential that he might not. After all, he was only eight years old at the time, and we only had a few short conversations over the course of a couple of weeks. While Billy had certainly left an indelible mark on my life, it was impossible for me to know what kind of mark I had made on him. Somehow that thought was hurtful to me, and I managed to push it away for the rest of the evening. But as I waited outside his office the next morning, it once again began to work on me. Here I was so excited to talk to Billy, and he might not even know who I am.

For an instant I considered leaving before he saw me, but I knew that was probably just the enemy trying to keep me from what could be a divine appointment. I prayed silently that God would bless our time together and immediately a wonderful sense of His peace rolled over me. Just as my body seemed to settle into the calm, Billy's door opened and my heart shifted back into high gear. Two very distinguished men walked out of his office and, just behind them, was Billy. As he stood in the doorway speaking to the secretary, I was amazed to see how tall he had gotten. I quickly stood to my feet, hoping that he would recognize me and when he turned my way, his face broke into a broad smile. Just as he had done in the district's hearing room twenty five years ago, Billy moved quickly across the reception area and in a surprisingly loud voice said, "Mr. Davis! It is so good to see you!" When he got to where I was standing, he threw his arms around me like an old friend, and I hugged back as though he was my own son. The strong paternal feelings that I had for him all those years ago came roaring back up in me. I had promised myself that I wouldn't cry, but tears of joy flowed anyway. It was a moment that I will always cherish.

VIII. Turning Back the Years

Billy led me into his office, which didn't look at all like I imagined it would. With all of the amazing things that he'd accomplished I expected to see the walls covered in diplomas and awards, but instead they were covered in pictures and souvenirs, which appeared to be from his extensive travels. There were pictures that appeared to have been drawn by small children, there were handwritten notes, there were photographs of Billy with people who appeared to live in Third World countries and with people who appeared to be mentally handicapped and with many other people that I couldn't identify. All of them were wonderfully preserved in frames, as though each were a treasure. The shelves were not filled with books, but instead with more memorabilia from his life, much of which looked homemade. Other than the computer, the phone, and some filing cabinets, there was little that wouldn't be at home in someone's living room.

As I looked around the room I realized that Billy hadn't set this room up to impress anyone, but, instead, to remind himself of what was valuable to him. He was a "people" person and he found value in the relationships that he'd had along the way. These walls silently conveyed his testimony to everyone who entered. I caught myself wanting to know the story behind each piece of memorabilia, but I resisted the urge to ask. Billy led me to what appeared to be a sitting area, with a couple of high-backed chairs and a small couch, where he told me to make myself comfortable. I caught myself staring at him as he pulled a couple of cold bottles of water from a small refrigerator, which was cleverly disguised as a filing cabinet. While I marveled at the change in his physical appearance, something about his countenance seemed completely unchanged. Even as a distinguished, accomplished man in his thirties, I sensed childlike enthusiasm and wonder in him. He not only didn't seem to be trying to impress me, he legitimately didn't seem all that impressed with himself. He smiled as he caught me staring at him, and he handed me a bottle of water as he sat in the chair across from me.

"It's incredible to see you after all these years. You haven't changed a bit," he began.

"Well, that's nice of you to say, but, truthfully, just about every-thing has changed since I last saw you."

With a big smile he said, "I suppose that it has."

"How is your mother doing?"

"I'm sorry to say that my mother went home to be with the Lord a couple of years ago."

I immediately regretted starting the conversation with that question and found myself surprisingly emotional at the news that she was gone. Though our association had been brief, her influence on my life had been significant. Even twenty five years later, I still remembered little pieces of wisdom she'd shared in our conversations. I don't think I ever encountered anyone who spoke more profoundly than she did. I definitely didn't want to put a damper on our conversation, but I knew it would be impossible to avoid speaking of her.

"I'm so sorry, Billy, or would you prefer I call you Dr. Turner?"

"'Billy' is fine, and like I say, she's with the Lord. I miss her a lot, but I know that I was blessed to have her as long as I did."

"If you don't mind me asking, what caused her to pass at such a young age?"

"It was ovarian cancer."

"Really, they're normally very successful in fighting that type of cancer."

"Yes, but because my mother was a nurse, she could always talk herself out of going to see a doctor. By the time they found it, she was in the final stages."

"She was such an amazing lady, it seems so sad that her life would be cut short."

"It's funny, because we talked about that a lot toward the end. She'd really lived a couple of lifetimes in fifty years. I don't know if she ever told you about her background, but both her parents were alcoholics and very abusive. She ran away from home at sixteen and was pregnant with me when she was eighteen. My dad's family was as big a mess as hers was, so they just clung to each other. She came to the Lord in the hospital, after they told her that I was dead in her womb. She prayed to God and said that if the Lord would spare me, she'd live the rest of her life for Him. Obviously, He did and as you know, she did as well."

"That's incredible. I never would have guessed that was your mother's background. She seemed so calm and wise. I just assumed that she grew up in church. Did she believe that the Lord brought you back to life or did she think that the doctor's had just made a mistake?"

"She said it didn't matter because it was a miracle either way. In the end she was saved and I was healthy."

"Yes, that sounds like your mother."

"Even though she and my father were married, he battled his alcoholism for years, so she pretty much had to raise me by herself. Though my dad was a hard worker, he drank up most of his paycheck, so mom eventually put herself through nursing school while I was still a baby. Of course, getting me to adulthood proved to be a much bigger challenge than anyone could have predicted and, then, to wind up with cancer, too. As hard as it was to let her go, I could see how tired she was, and I'm glad that she's finally able to rest."

"It sounds as though she had a very hard life."

"I'd say it was, but she genuinely considered herself to be very blessed. She said that despite her childhood, she still found the Lord as a teenager. Despite being told that she'd lost her baby, here I was, healthy and grown. Despite my father's alcoholism, he'd never been abusive and eventually recovered. Despite the tough years of their marriage, he really did love her, and before he passed, she was able to lead him to the Lord. Despite the struggles that I had with school, she'd lived to see me get my doctorate; and despite getting cancer at fifty, she'd lived to see all of her dreams come true."

I could almost hear her voice as Billy echoed her words. Her relentless hope in the face of adversity and her unwillingness to fall into self-pity convicted me. I'd suffered little or nothing in my life and yet I was still prone to throw myself the occasional pity party or to harbor wrong attitudes about my situation. I marveled at the remarkable life and death of this amazing woman and at the incredible son that she raised.

"I guess that sort of answers another question that I'd had for all these years."

"What's that?" Billy replied.

"I always wondered why your father hadn't been there to help during your trouble with the school. I guess his alcoholism kept him away."

"Not really, by then he was starting to get his life under control."

"Then what was it that kept him away?" I asked.

"It was the whole issue of spirituality. At that point he didn't really believe in any of that, and I'm not sure that he didn't think that maybe there was something wrong with me. Whenever he'd drink, he'd always withdraw from mom and me; he'd go out into the garage for hours or sometimes into the basement. We always knew to leave him alone. Years later when we were able to talk about it, he explained how his father used to get drunk and curse him and throw things at him. He said that he lived in fear that he'd find out that he was just like his father. Even after he quit drinking, he'd still withdraw from us when things got tense. I remember the day of the hearing, he was all dressed to go and, at the last minute, he just went out to the garage."

"Did that hurt you?"

"Not really, in my mind that was just his way. I think that it bothered my mom, but she just sighed and we went on."

"Did you and your father eventually become close?"

"You know, I always felt close to my father. He wasn't one to say much, but I'd just crawl up in his lap, and he'd wrap his arms around me. It was a great feeling. I somehow sensed that things were overwhelming to him, and so I picked my times, but I don't remember him ever turning me away."

"How did he react to the school district's decision to remove you from regular classes?"

"He seemed to stew about it for awhile. I think that he wanted to blame my mom for that whole mess. But if he did, I never heard it. I guess the thing that I'll always remember from that time is coming home from one of my Special Ed. field trips, where someone had called me a retard. I was so mad and hurt by it that I couldn't stop crying. My dad motioned for me to come to him, and he wrapped his arms around me, and he whispered in my ear, 'There isn't one thing wrong with you, son, and if people don't understand you it's their problem, not yours.' It was so out of character for him to offer consolation with words or to be openly defensive for me. It did something for my heart that no one else could have done. It was a vote of confidence from the person that I most needed it from. It's funny because my mother had fought tooth and nail for me every step of the way, but whenever I've doubted myself, it is that moment with my father that I've drawn back to."

"So you say that he eventually came to Christ?"

"Yes, the longer he stayed sober, the more his heart seemed to soften toward God. I think that both mom and I thought he'd make that choice a lot sooner than he did, but when I was in college my mom called me with the news. I remember the first time we all prayed together. I just couldn't stop crying and thanking God. When he decided to get baptized, he asked the pastor if I could be the one to do it. It was one of the greatest moments of my life."

Billy was moved to tears, and it was impossible for me to not be moved there with him.

"It's amazing to think of how my parents grew up. There was no kindhearted grandma to sneak them off to Vacation Bible School. No sweet aunt in the background, secretly praying for their souls, and yet, God was still able to draw them to Himself. It is testimony to me of His amazing grace and sovereignty."

"You're so right, Billy, and wrapped within that is the story of my own salvation. Here I had been raised in church, with little or no effect, yet the witness of an eight year old boy and his mother changed everything for me. It is amazing to consider the patience and wisdom of God."

"Yes, it is," Billy replied with a wistful smile.

We silently lingered in the moment before continuing.

"How about some lunch, Mr. Davis?"

"Well, I don't want to be an imposition."

"Oh, please, when I heard you were coming, I cleared my schedule for the rest of the afternoon."

"Really? I must confess that I was wondering if you'd even remember who I was."

"How could I forget?"

"You were only eight years old."

"Yes, but that was a turning point in my life."

"I imagine that it was very traumatic."

"Interestingly, I don't really remember feeling that way. I could see the profound effect it was having on the people around us, but I guess I didn't really understand the implications of it all. My mother seemed very calm, and so I assumed that everything was going to be OK."

"Well, I'd be lying if I said that I wasn't dying to hear the rest of the story, so by all means, let's get some lunch."

IX. Aftermath

As someone who spent his entire career observing the behavior patterns of children, I found it fascinating to watch Billy move about the adult world. While he had no doubt matured, he was still very much the "people person" that he'd always been. He spoke to everyone that we encountered in the same warm and friendly manner. There was no visible change in his countenance, regardless of whether he was speaking to his secretary, to a student who stopped him in the hall, to the head of the Education Department who we saw in the parking lot, or to the waiter at our lunch table. He seemed to be refreshingly free of pretension. Though he dressed sharply, his clothes were not "designer". In a faculty parking lot full of Lexus' and BMW's, he drove a Honda sedan. The restaurant that he chose for lunch was nice, but not particularly affluent. If he was making any sort of effort to keep up appearances, it was indiscernible.

I couldn't wait to get back to the story of what had happened to him after being removed from the school district, but before I could ask, he asked me about my own story. We spent a lot more time with that than I really wanted to, but Billy seemed genuinely interested, and so I shared it with him. We were finished with lunch and having some coffee before we got back to Billy's story.

"I'd be very interested to hear about what happened after the hearing with the school district."

"Well, as you know they turned the whole matter over to the

State School Board, so I spent months being evaluated for what they called, "placement." Based on Dr. Smith's report from the hearing, they decided that I had attention deficit disorder, severe learning disabilities, bi-polar disorder and a mild form of schizophrenia, characterized by paranoid delusion."

"My Lord, did they really believe all that?"

"I guess. They prescribed all sorts of medication, none of which my mother ever got for me, and I was placed in a class with other mentally disabled kids."

"That must have been terrible."

"You know, at first it wasn't a big deal to me. Most of the kids were very nice, and the staff people were far more patient than my regular teachers had been. I was what they called, 'high functioning,' so there was very little pressure for me, and I really liked helping the other kids. But from the beginning my mother was intent on getting me out of there. You know, that was before the whole home school movement took hold, so she was required to petition the state for permission to teach me at home. They made it very tough on her, and it took almost three years for the petition to be approved."

"You said it wasn't a big deal at first. Did things change during those three years?"

"Absolutely, it was really strange, but the longer I was identified with that group, the more I started to breakdown."

"Breakdown?"

"Yes, I'd go through these episodes where I'd fall into this almost autistic state, suddenly feeling exhausted, filled with confusion and unable to put my thoughts together. I could hear people speaking to me, but was unable to respond. It was like being underwater with my hands and feet tied together. Though the episodes normally didn't last very long, it would sometimes take days for me to feel normal again. They began to push the issue of medication with my mother, but she knew that it was a spiritual issue. As long as she was around, she'd just come against the spirits that were attacking me. Unfortunately, she couldn't be with me twenty four hours a day and these things tended to come on me at school. I certainly knew how to pray against demons, but somehow I was never able to discern the onset of these episodes and was totally incapacitated once they started.

For awhile, there was a staff member at the school who understood spiritual things and was able to intercede on my behalf. But one day when she wasn't around, I slipped into one of these episodes and no one knew what to do. After several minutes, I began to convulse, and by the time the rescue squad arrived I was having a full-blown seizure. When my mom arrived at the emergency room, they told her that they thought I might have had a brain aneurysm, but could offer no explanation for the array of symptoms I displayed (e.g. difficulty breathing, choking…) or why those symptoms suddenly disappeared, even before I was heavily sedated. It was only after my mother saw a lady that we knew from church and who happened to be on duty in the ER when I came in, that she got the real story. This lady told her that as they wheeled me in the door she'd had a vision of a huge lizard on my head.

It had its claws digging into the top of my skull, and its tail completely wrapped around my throat. When she saw that, she gathered a couple of the other nurses, and they began praying against it. By the time they came to sedate me, the seizure was over, and I'd passed out from exhaustion. I think that this incident really scared the people at the school, and it wasn't long after that episode that they granted my mother's petition to teach me at home."

"It sounds like it was awful."

"Well, it's like pretty much everything that you encounter in this life. It had its challenges and its blessings. I made some life-long friends in those years and gained some valuable insight into the way special needs kids are handled in the education system. A big part of my desire to get into the education field and to get involved with education reform came from that experience. I don't know if you've ever been around people that they classify as mentally handicapped, but whatever they may lack in the natural doesn't seem to hinder their spirits. They seem to laugh easily, and to cry easily, and to love easily, and to forgive easily. They often seem blessedly disconnected from many of the vices that drag our souls down, and I can't help but wonder if we who have all our temporal faculties intact aren't really the handicapped ones."

"I see your point. I guess I never really considered it that way."

"My only lament from that time is how difficult it was on my mother. I wish that she could have been spared some of that."

"I doubt that she'd complain," I asserted.

"Of course, you're right. She always said that her main mission in life was to get me to my destiny, and, as much as any human can, she did that."

"So, I imagine that home school was quite a relief from the special education program?"

"Well, spiritually it was a lot better. I never had another one of those episodes or seizures, but I didn't really like it at first. I liked being with people, and being at home while everyone else was at school was not my idea of fun. I did like my Mom being the teacher, and I liked the fact that I could go really fast and get done early, but I really wanted to be with my friends.

It was a struggle for the first six months, but we eventually developed a routine and I started doing better than I ever had in school."

"Judging from where you've landed, you must have been a tremendous student."

"Not always. My struggle wasn't in understanding things; the problem for me was staying focused. But Mom was able to tell when I was drifting, and she figured out ways to help me get back on track."

"Like what?"

"She'd break long segments of reading or writing into smaller blocks and mix them up with interactive stuff. Like when we were learning about hydraulics, she took me down to the tire store and got one of the mechanics to show me how the car lift worked. He even let me run it up and down a few times. That kind of stuff really worked me, and she never seemed short of ideas about how to make a principle tangible for me. I remember one time we spent a whole afternoon watching them demolish these old high-rise tenement buildings. For the life of me, I can't remember how she tied that into school, but I remember being fascinated by the whole process. She made learning seem like an adventure, and I was always up for an adventure."

"It's incredible that she was able to devote that kind of energy and work nights, too!"

"It is incredible. We would go to the library all of the time, and I always had about twenty things checked out. I learned how to get lost in a book, and reading stopped being such a struggle. If we had some place to go, we'd go first thing in the morning, after she'd get off work. After lunch I'd normally do my reading and writing stuff, while Mom would try to sleep for a few hours. After a couple of years, we had a really good system, and she didn't have to stay on me all of the time."

"I read where you graduated early, how did that come about?"

"Well, the school district was always putting Mom through it about whether I was getting an adequate education and so I had to be tested at the end of every year. By my junior high years I was doing so well on those tests that they started having me evaluated by a 'special education advisor.' She became so convinced that I was some sort of prodigy that she arranged for me to take the SAT at the end of my ninth grade year. When I scored better than that year's valedictorian, they stopped talking about the quality of my education. Though I did do my tenth grade year at home, I started taking classes at the college as well. That next summer I got my GED and was a full time college student that fall. Though my mother was the least prideful person that I've ever known, I got a sense that she allowed herself to take a little satisfaction in proving the school system wrong. Ironically, they never did take that "Special Ed" designation off of my record, which I suppose gives me the dubious distinction of being one of the few mentally impaired students to earn his doctorate."

"I guess that would put you in pretty rare company."

"It always makes me think of that verse that says that the 'wisdom of men is foolishness to God.'"

"Amen. It also makes me think of Mike Skinner. I wonder if anyone ever told him about how things turned out with you."

"It's ironic that you'd mention his name because I've got some things to share with you that involve him. But before we go any further, I thought I'd ask about your wife."

"Well, I think I pretty much told you that story."

"No, no. I mean it's gotten pretty late, won't she be expecting you back?"

I had to admit that he was right, but I felt like a giddy school boy and I wasn't ready for this conversation to stop. I had such a profound sense of God's sovereignty as the story of Billy's life unfolded. It validated everything that I'd come to believe about how God works through circumstances and or-chestrates His will despite our stubbornness. I remembered my deep feelings of failure about this incident and seeing "Dr. William Turner" was like a big punchbowl of redemption. Somehow his overcoming felt like affirmation to me, and his victory felt as though it were my victory, too. The hours we had spent together were like some sort of spiritual high, and I wasn't ready to come down. There was still so much to talk about. So much that I still wanted to know. But Billy was right, and I knew that I needed to get back to Katherine.

"She will be expecting me, and I have no right to ask this of you, but would you consider having dinner with us? There is so much that I'd still like to talk about."

"Well, it's funny that you should ask, because I was going to ask you the same thing. I'm supposed to meet with two very special people tonight, and we could just make that a table for five."

"Oh, I don't want to disrupt your plans for the evening," I said.

Billy's expression became serious as he asked, "Mr. Davis, do you believe in 'Divine Appointments'?"

"Of course, I do," I replied.

"I believe that this dinner may very well be one of those ap-pointments for all five of us."

As he spoke, I felt the hair on my arms rise up and a tin-gling running down my spine. I got the sense that there was something that he wasn't telling me, but I had already come to the conclusion that this whole thing had been orchestrated by God. So I decided against asking for an explanation. Af-ter getting directions for our dinner meeting, we exchanged a warm hug and all of those paternal feelings came flooding in again. I was so proud of him that I felt like I would burst. Tears streamed down my face and my heart was overflowing as I headed back the hotel and to my precious Katherine.

X. The Man of My Dreams

As I approached the door to our hotel room, a twinge of guilt cut through the adrenaline rush that had accompanied the last several hours. Katherine and I were rarely apart for any amount of time, and it bothered me that I'd left her alone all afternoon. I knew that she would understand, but it gnawed at me, anyway. As I unlocked the door, it flashed through my mind that I should probably just cancel dinner with Billy and his special friends and devote the entire evening to my Katherine. I rationalized that Billy was probably just being polite in inviting us anyway and by the time I stepped through the door, I had already resolved in my mind that I would cancel.

Katherine greeted me warmly, but I could immediately tell that something was wrong. She looked tired and troubled. I wondered if maybe she was angry with me or if she had been worrying, but she insisted that she was fine. She diverted me away from my questions by asking about my afternoon, which got me rolling at warp speed through all of the stories. Seeing my excitement seemed to brighten her some, but I could tell that something was eating at her. Even in the midst of my excitement, I had to stop and ask her again.

"Please, Katherine, tell me what's wrong?"

She let out a heavy sigh and said, "Oh, Bob, it's nothing important, just some silly dreams."

"Dreams?" I replied.

"Yes, I was reading earlier, and I got so sleepy that I decided to take a little nap. You know that I'm not one to dream, but I had two of the most vivid dreams I've ever had, and they both left me feeling strange."

"'Strange', in what way?"

"I don't know. Disturbed, I guess. I got the sense that both of these dreams were supposed to mean something to me, but for the life of me, I don't what," she said.

"Well, tell me about them."

"In the first dream, I was driving through a residential area by myself and it seemed to be late at night. I suddenly noticed that one of the houses was on fire. I stopped the car and started fumbling around for my cell phone, when I saw a man walking from the burning house. It was so odd, because he seemed very calm, and he didn't appear to have been affected by the fire at all. He wasn't sweating or covered in soot from the smoke. I jumped out of the car and asked him if he was alright, but he just stared at me and kept walking. As he passed me I asked if there was anyone else in the house, which caused him to stop and stare at me some more. His face seemed totally devoid of expression, and he didn't say a word. Just at that moment, I heard screams coming from inside the house, and I spun around to see if someone needed help. When I couldn't see anyone, I turned back to the man to tell him that we needed to do something, but he was gone. That's how the dream ended."

"When you say 'gone', do you mean, like, he disappeared?" I queried.

"I don't know, he was just gone."

"Do you think he was the one who set the fire?"

"I don't know, Bob! I really have no idea what to make of it, but it has really haunted me this afternoon. I get the nagging feeling that it means something, but I don't know what."

"Me neither, though it reminds of yet another part of this whole Billy Turner story," I added.

"Really?"

"Yes, did I ever tell you what became of Jared Lowe?"

"Not that I remember."

"I guess I have to start by admitting that most of what I know about this is secondhand, because the Lowes moved out of the school district shortly after the hearing. But I've heard from several people in the district's administration office that the Lowes accepted a large cash settlement to keep the case out of court. They moved to somewhere around Los Angeles, and I figured that would be the last we'd hear of them. But a few years later I saw on the news where their house had burned down, with Jared's parents and another couple inside. Within a couple of days they arrested Jared and charged him with arson and murder."

"Oh, Lord, it's just like what Billy had sensed on the playground," Katherine gasped.

"That's right, and during the trial details of the horrible abuse that Jared had been enduring came out. It was even worse than I'd imagined. Apparently his parents and the other couple that died in the fire, had been drunk and molesting the boy that night."

Tears began to stream down Katherine's cheeks as she whispered, "Oh, dear God!"

I could feel the tears welling up in my eyes too, as I remembered Jared sitting between his parents at the hearing. Fresh waves of anger swept over me as I thought about how Mike Skinner had become an unwitting accomplice to this horrible tragedy, though I doubted that he would be willing to accept any responsibility for it.

"Surely the courts understood that, under the circumstances, it was a matter of self defense?" Katherine pleaded.

"I guess that they must have considered it, because they did reduce the charges and apparently struck some sort of deal with Jared's lawyers. Nonetheless, I heard that he did spend time in both psychiatric hospitals and in prison. Because he was a juvenile the court records were sealed, and I never really heard what became of him after that. Considering how damaged he was at nine years old, I can't imagine what would be left of him after all that's happened in the years since then."

For the next few minutes Katherine and I sat in silence. All of the exhilaration of the day had now left me, as I considered the destruction of this little boy. I remembered what Mrs. Turner had said about the open spiritual doorways into Jared's life, and my heart ached at the thought of how little I had prayed for him. I was wondering if Billy knew anything more about Jared's fate, when Katherine broke the silence.

"I don't think my dream was about Jared," she said.

"Why not?"

"Because, it was a man coming out of the fire and not a little boy. Besides I sense this dream has more to do with the future than the past."

"You're probably right, but what you described just reminded me of Jared's story. So, what about the other dream?" I asked.

"Well, it was much shorter. It was just this courtroom scene with what appeared to be the defense lawyer, making a very passionate argument."

"So what is so disturbing about that?"

"What bothered me was that you and I were sitting at the defense table."

As I pictured it in my mind, I asked, "You mean, like, we were the defendants?"

"That's what it looked like to me. We didn't seem to be anxious in the dream, but ever since I woke up I've been wracking my brain to come up with a scenario in which this could be a good thing."

"I can understand that, but maybe it's not meant to be viewed literally," I suggested.

"Well, even if you look at it symbolically, it doesn't seem very good," she replied.

"I guess I see your point, but we can't let ourselves be too worried about it. If God's trying to tell us something, He'll get through to us when He needs to."

"I know that you're right, and it ought to be easier now that you're back, since I won't have to be alone with my thoughts."

I explained to Katherine about Billy's dinner invitation and my willingness to back out if necessary. But I had to admit that talking about Jared Lowe had brought me back to the place of really wanting to go. It turned out that she'd been hoping for such an invitation, as she really wanted to meet Billy for herself. I loved that she'd been willing to give me the space to be alone with Billy all afternoon; even though it could have meant that she wouldn't get the chance to meet him. It was typical of Katherine's unselfish way of thinking, and I felt incredibly blessed to have her as a partner. It didn't take her any time at all to get ready, and as we left the hotel I caught myself thanking God for who He'd made her to be and for allowing me to share my life with her.

When we got the restaurant the foyer was crowded, and I wasn't sure whether Billy had arrived yet. As we stood in line to speak to the hostess Katherine was loosely holding on to my arm, when I suddenly felt her clutch tightly. When I turned to look at her face, she looked as if she'd seen a ghost.

"What's the matter, honey?" I asked in a loud whisper.

"It's him!" she answered in a similar voice.

"Who?"

"That man over there, the one the hostess is taking to the table," she gasped.

I barely caught a glimpse of the back of the man's head before he disappeared into the restaurant with the hostess. "So who is he?" I asked numbly.

Turning to me, she said, "He's the man from my dream!"

"You mean, the burning house dream?"

"Yes!"

A surge of electricity came spiraling through my body, as I was suddenly aware that this was, in fact, a divine appointment. I shuddered at the thought of how close I had come to cancelling the whole evening. Part of me wanted to walk through the restaurant to find this man, but the still small voice inside of me let me know that it wouldn't be necessary.

"What should we do?" Katherine asked breathlessly.

"I get the sense that we won't have to do anything. I can feel God's hand on this and I'm sure He'll bring it together in His own way."

Katherine seemed to exhale the tension of the moment and said, "I'm sure you're right."

After a few more minutes of waiting, we reached the hostess stand and she finally led us through the restaurant, in the same direction she'd taken the mystery man. I wasn't even a little bit surprised when we found him sitting with Billy as we reached the table. As they both rose to their feet, I got my first good look at him and something about him seemed familiar, but I couldn't place it. Something in his eyes told me that he knew me, and so I decided to try to head off an awkward moment.

"Gentlemen, this is my beautiful wife, Katherine."

Billy immediately stepped forward and gently took Katherine's hand. "It is such a pleasure to meet you, Mrs. Davis, I've heard many wonderful things about you."

Katherine smiled graciously and said, "The pleasure is mine, Mr. Turner, and, please, call me Katherine."

Billy smiled warmly and replied, "Only if you'll call me William, or Billy, if you'd like."

Katherine again nodded in agreement.

As Billy backed up a step, he casually added, "And I'm sure

that Mr. Davis will remember our friend, Jared."

Despite the fact that I had sensed that something was coming, I couldn't harness my shock at the revelation that the young man standing in front of me was none other than Jared Lowe. It was a moment not unlike my first glimpse of "Dr. William Turner." I couldn't recognize him because in my mind I pictured him as a tormented soul. I expected a crumpled shell of a human being and never imagined that he could be anything like the well dressed, clear eyed, ruggedly handsome young man standing next to Billy.

Once again, I was struck by the awesomeness of God and His sovereignty. I totally lost consciousness of social graces, as a wave of paternal feelings once again flooded my heart. I could see that Jared was measuring my response with his eyes and waiting for me to make the first move, which I did, without reservation.

With tears in my eyes and my heart feeling like it would burst, I stepped toward him.

"My God, son, it is so good to see you," I said, as I threw my arms around him. I could tell that he wasn't quite ready for that, as his embrace was tentative at first. But as I held him tight, I felt him melt into it. When I finally was able to let him go, I could see that there were tears in his eyes as well.

"It's good to see you, too, Mr. Davis," he said quietly.

I could see that Jared's hand was shaking as he tentatively extended it toward Katherine. And I could see in her face that she fully understood the gravity of the moment. "I'm so glad to meet you, Jared," she said, as she firmly grasped his hand. I got the sense that our warm welcome was something of a relief to Jared, and it dawned on me that he'd wondered whether we might reject him. That thought caused yet another wave of emotion to spill over me, though I was able to suppress my urge to wrap my arms around him again. Unfortunately, I wasn't able to suppress my urge to stare at him in wonder. Unlike when they were children, Billy now stood a head taller than Jared, though Jared did appear to be more powerfully built. Though his dark hair and some of his features were not surprising as I remembered his parents, nothing in his overall appearance seemed to evoke them. Though he was clearly a young man, something in his face made him appear to be years older than Billy. Thankfully, Billy pulled me back into the present as he said, "Why don't we sit down?"

Before I could even take a step toward the table, Billy had pulled out a chair for Katherine, who seemed utterly charmed by his manners. She smiled broadly as she sat down and said, "Thank you, Mr. Turner." To which he quickly replied, "You're quite welcome, Mrs. Davis." Katherine blushed as she realized that she'd already forgotten their agreement about using first names. I slid into the chair between Katherine and Jared, while Billy sat between Jared and the empty chair that awaited our other mystery guest.

As Billy picked up his menu he said, "Our other guest, MJ, is running late tonight, so let's go ahead and order before we start catching up on the last few years." As I glanced at the menu I wondered if Billy was trying to tell me not to probe too far with Jared or whether his use of the phrase "the last few years" was simply incidental. I understood that Jared's past had to be difficult for him, but I couldn't help but wonder how he had emerged from this seemingly hopeless situation. While I had resolved not to probe too deeply I hoped that Jared would feel the need to explain, and after we'd all ordered, I did what I could to get that conversation started.

"I can't begin to tell you what a surprise it is to see you! When Billy mentioned having dinner, he didn't let me in on who his other guests would be."

"So, he hasn't said anything about MJ either?" Jared asked.

"No, he sure hasn't," I replied with an incredulous smile.

Billy smiled back, as he replied, "In my defense, we were still doing a lot of catching up today, and we hadn't really gotten into the present tense yet."

"Likely story," Jared shot back with a smirk.

It was clear from their playful exchange that Billy and Jared had developed a genuine friendship somewhere along the way, which only served to piqué my curiosity. I couldn't resist the urge to try to move the conversation back in that direction, so I asked, "So how is it that you two crossed paths after all these years?"

Katherine shot me a brief, but uneasy glance, which let me know that I was probably a little out of line with that question. I'd learned to trust her judgment in these kinds of situations, but it was too late to pull it back. I saw Billy look at Jared, with an expression that seemed to convey his willingness to answer the question, but Jared's expression seemed to let Billy know that it wouldn't be necessary. Jared's eyes seemed to fix on the salt and pepper shakers in front of him, as he began to speak quietly.

"I guess I need to go back to the beginning," he said.

To which Katherine compassionately added, "Jared, you don't have to talk about this if you don't want to."

But Jared's glance rose to meet Katherine's as he said, "No, I think that it is important that we go all the way back, so that we'll be able to move forward."

I didn't really understand what Jared meant about moving forward, and I was proud of Katherine for the grace that she'd extended him, but, above all, I was glad that he was willing to share his story with us. I was a little ashamed of myself for feeling that way, but eager enough to live with that. Jared's glance locked back in on the salt shaker, which he was now rolling between his fingers, and his voice took on a low tone of resignation as he began to speak.

"Things were always rough at home when I was growing up. They started out bad and grew steadily worse. My father was mean and a drug addict; my mother was also into drugs and too afraid of my father to protect me. For as long as I can remember, he'd just explode and start beating on my mother. He'd call her every name in the book and accuse her of being with other men. When I was about five years old I decided I should try to defend her, but when I did, he beat me even worse than he did her. Once it happened that first time, it became an everyday thing. Sometimes I'd just be sitting there and he'd put his cigarette out on my arm or on my head. If I made a sound he'd become enraged and start punching or kicking me. Until I got too big to pick up, he liked to throw me against the wall or onto things he knew would hurt me.

He was also a pervert, who liked to watch porn movies all the time and who expected my mother to do the things he saw in those movies. He started bringing men home with him and made my mother do things to them as well. Afterwards he'd beat her for being with them. I begged my mom to leave him and to take me with her, but she was convinced that he'd find us and kill us. I remember thinking that being dead didn't seem like such a bad thing."

Jared's voice trailed off and his eyes slowly rose from the table, as if to see whether we were still there. Billy's face was filled with compassion and Katherine's eyes were moist with tears. I now felt greatly ashamed that I'd wanted him to share this so badly without really considering what it might cost him to revisit those memories.

"I'm sorry if this is too graphic," he said. "It just kind of explains what came next."

My gut was wrenched with emotion as I said, "Jared, you don't need to do this for us."

But as he looked me in the eye he said, "I think that I should. I think that the only way for me to stay free of this is to not be afraid of talking about it. Besides, I think that there is reason we've all come together again, and we won't be able to go forward unless the truth comes out."

I could feel the tears welling up in my eyes as I considered the bravery of this young man. I doubt that I could have survived what he was describing, much less talk about it openly. Jared's eyes once again fell to his fidgeting hands as he began to speak.

"I really didn't see how things could get worse, but I can remember the day they did. My father got a hold of some porn tapes from Mexico that had children in them. I remember him yelling for me from the living room and when I saw what he was watching, I knew what was going to happen. The day after that first time was the day that Billy came to me on the playground. I was so in anguish that day and if I could have taken it out on him, I might have killed him. I now understand that the power inside of him that day was far more powerful than the forces working on me."

As the tears rolled down my face, I remembered sitting with Jared in my office, as he tried to explain that, for some reason, he couldn't seem to stop Billy that day, and how Billy's prayers had made him feel "calm." As I considered what that little boy was enduring at the time, I gained a new appreciation for just how miraculous it was for him to have felt that way. I also began to realize that, whether I understood it or not, God must have been speaking to me as well. I'd never heard any stories about Jared's family, and I'd never seen a bruise on him, yet somehow I had sensed this abuse, even the sexual nature of it. As I tried to think of where that idea might have come from, I couldn't come up with anything other than divine intervention.

But just as the magnitude of that moment washed over me, so did the guilt of my failure to help Jared. The realization that

I'd known this in my heart and that I'd done nothing to stop it, was almost more than I could bear. I found myself gasping for air as my emotions overwhelmed me. I laid my head on my hands, which were resting on the table, and I began to weep.

The profound sense of failure was crushing and I felt like the worst kind of coward for choosing to protect my career instead of this defenseless little boy. It seemed to erase every good thing I'd accomplished in all my years of working with children. Though I was aware that I was probably making a spectacle of myself, I couldn't seem to suppress these thoughts and emotions. I tried desperately to regain my composure, but wave after wave seemed to come upon me. I could hear Katherine asking me what was the matter, but I couldn't seem to gather myself long enough to answer her.

It was feeling Jared's strong hand on my back that seemed to slow my tailspin, as I felt the need to beg for his forgiveness. As I pulled my head off the table and turned towards him, I could see that he was kneeling on one knee, next to my chair. I could tell that he was somewhat bewildered by my sudden emotional outburst, and that he was sincerely concerned. As our eyes met, he was the first to speak.

"What is it, Mr. Davis?"

Though I meant to speak softly, my emotions caused the words to come out with more volume than I intended.

"I knew, Jared!" I cried.

"I knew, in my heart, that they were destroying you, and I did nothing to stop it!"

"I should have stopped them!"

"I'm so sorry that I didn't stop them!" I sobbed.

"Please forgive me for being such a coward!" I gurgled through my tears.

Jared's expression became pained, as he reached his hand to my face and, with an almost stern voice, said, "No! Don't you do that!"

"You might have known in your heart, but you could never have proven anything. If you would have made that accusation, I would have been too scared to admit it, and you'd have had no evidence. It would have cost you your career, and it would only have made things worse for me."

"Don't let that voice in your head! There was nothing you could have done," he declared firmly.

As we fell into an embrace I continued to weep, but now it was for the hurt that this little boy had known. Just as quickly as those feelings of guilt had swarmed around me, Jared's words had scattered them. I immediately knew that what he'd said was true and that there really was nothing that I could have done. I'd always recognized my sense of failure for not being of more help to Billy, but I'd never understood the burden of guilt that I'd carried all those years for Jared, as well. As painful as the truth was, it had once again set me free.

As the emotion of the moment ebbed I regained my composure, as Katherine gently stroked my shoulder, and Jared returned to his chair. Apparently, as Katherine and Billy had witnessed this exchange between Jared and me, they had joined hands and begun to pray. I was amazed at the instant bond they seemed to have formed, and once again that tingling sensation that God's hand was on all of this returned. After the waiter dropped off our drinks, Jared continued.

"After the incident with Billy my father left me alone for awhile. I think that he was afraid that someone might get to me. He pretended to be worried about me, but he was really just looking for a way to work the system. For the couple of months that whole thing at school went on, he didn't touch me once. Of course, my mom got it even worse during that time. She kept telling me that things had changed, but I could watch my father and know that they hadn't. After he got the settlement money and we moved, he picked back up right where he left off, and within a few months, things were worse than I ever could have imagined.

I tried to run away a couple of times, but I never got very far, and my father always made me pay for it. Eventually, I felt just like my mother, powerless and too afraid to leave. I remember lying in my bed at night and fantasizing about dying. I even remember praying at times. I wasn't sure that there was a God, but I was willing to try anything. Every day that I woke up in that house, it convinced me that either there was no God, or, if there was, that He was as twisted as my father."

As Jared stopped to sip his water, I could see that there were once again no dry eyes around the table. Billy now appeared as distraught as Katherine and I had been. I was almost afraid to drink my water for fear that I wouldn't be able to keep it down. As badly as I had wanted to hear the story, I now wished that I didn't know. For Jared's sake, I knew that he needed to finish the story, and so I prayed that the Lord would help us all to get through it.

"On the night of the fire, my parents had another couple over. They were getting high and making plans for the future. This man made dirty movies, and his specialty was child pornography. He seemed to be showing my dad the ropes by demonstrating on me. I kept trying to crawl back to my bedroom, but my father would catch me and force me to stay in the room with them. All the lights were out and the room was filled with lit candles. It was hot and smoky from all the pot they were smoking. It was hard to breathe, and at some point I must have passed out. When I woke up, the room seemed even hotter and smokier than before, and I laid there for a few minutes before I once again tried to get back to my bedroom. It wasn't until I crawled to the hallway that I actually looked back and saw that the living room was on fire.

At first, I really believed that I must be dreaming. I didn't immediately jump up, because the thought of being consumed by the fire seemed somehow appealing. For awhile, I just laid there and watched the fire, never really considering that there were people dying in the room. For a long time all I could hear was the rushing wind sound of the fire, but eventually the sound of my mother's screams reached my ears. Her pain was the one thing that still had the power to move me, and realizing that she was in the midst of the fire sent a surge of electricity through my body. I tried to pull myself up and see her through the smoke, but by then the room was completely engulfed, and the heat was just too much to bear. I tried to call back to her, but the sound of my voice couldn't seem to overcome the roar of the fire. I grabbed a towel from the bathroom and tried to use it as a mask, but as I started back down the hall, I could feel the skin on my forehead blistering.

It was then that I heard my father's voice and saw that he had crawled to the hallway entrance. He was screaming for me to help him, and somehow, through the smoke, and the heat, and the flames, our eyes met. He was probably only ten feet from me, but it might as well have been miles. It was a surreal moment, and my blood ran cold. I wasn't filled with rage or even a little bit angry. I didn't think about all he'd done or that he was getting what he deserved. I just couldn't seem to muster any emotion at all, though I will admit that the thought of trying to save him did seem ridiculous to me. Somehow he understood that I wasn't going to help him, and he began to curse me, saying that if he got out of this, he'd kill me.

Even though a part of me knew that he had no power over this situation, another part of me wanted to panic at his words. I moved back into the bathroom and locked the door. The closed door muffled the sound of the fire, except for the crashing sounds that I assumed were parts of the house collapsing. My plan to allow the fire to consume me hadn't really changed at that point, but the realization that my father would likely perish opened up a new possibility for me. If he was gone, maybe I could go on. As I pondered that, I pulled on some dirty clothes from the hamper and decided to crawl out of the window. I wish I could tell you that when I got out I ran and went for help, but I didn't. I just started walking, and I never even looked back."

Jared once again paused and seemed to be looking for our reaction to his story. I sensed that he was relieved to find nothing but tearful eyes and sympathetic stares. I was again struck by the character of this young man. It would have been so easy for him to have told this story without sharing the parts that brought his motivations into question, but his honesty only made my respect for him grow. It was Katherine who was the first to speak.

"Didn't anyone see that the house was on fire, or question what had happened to you?"

"Honestly, Mrs. Davis, it was the middle of the night, and so I doubt that anyone saw much. I didn't see anyone until the next morning," replied Jared.

"Where did you go?" I added.

"There was an old practice field by the gym at my school. I used to hang out under the bleachers during lunchtime and smoke. I passed out there for awhile. When I woke up, I wondered if it had all been a dream, but from the smell of my clothes, I knew that it wasn't. I managed to break the padlock off one of the supply sheds and found some old practice uniforms in a box. I changed clothes and cleaned up as best I could. I figured that I'd try to get back to the San Diego area, because my mom had a sister there."

"Why not just go back home?" I continued.

"Because I didn't know whether my father had somehow survived, and I wasn't willing to take that chance," he said.

We again fell silent as the gravity of this story continued to resonate with each of us. My mind reeled as I imagined what it must have been like for a child to face this kind of ordeal. Though the story wasn't very different from what I'd heard, viewing it through Jared's eyes brought a stunning reality to it. Even though I knew better I caught myself entertaining the question of why God would allow such a thing, though I quickly reminded myself that the Garden of Eden was God's plan for us and that everything else was a by-product of man's fall. Nevertheless, the injustice of it all still gnawed at me. Jared eventually broke the silence and continued.

"I did make it to San Diego, and my aunt convinced me to go to the police. They had pretty much decided that I had torched the house, and so they immediately arrested me. They were pretty nasty at first, and since there were no eyewitnesses, it looked like I was done for. But, thankfully, my court-appointed lawyer knew what he was doing, and he was able to prod them into doing a real investigation. They weren't able to get much from what was left of our house, but the doctor's examination of me provided a lot of physical evidence, and a search of the other couple's home substantiated that my story was true. Though the district attorney eventually reduced the charges, he wasn't willing to let go of the fact that I didn't call for help, and I was found guilty of involuntary manslaughter.

Because of my age and the circumstances, I wasn't supposed to do any jail time, but they did have some serious concerns about my mental condition. So, I was placed in a state psychiatric hospital for further evaluation. The counselor there was really helping me to work through some things from the past, but there were also some staff members who were only making things worse. If a patient made them mad, they'd often sedate them and put them in restraints. At night I would hear things, and I believed that they were abusing some of the patients, but I knew I could never prove it. Hearing people cry out in the dark would stir up all my old fears, and I began to withdraw from the rehabilitation process. Once I got labeled as being 'non-cooperative,' the staff started working on me too. Sometimes they'd withhold food from me, and other times I'd get locked in my room.

As my anger grew, they started giving me shots and restraining me at night. One orderly in particular seemed to have it in for me, and one night, while I was restrained in my bed, he decided to come teach me a lesson. He shoved a sock in my mouth so that no one would hear me scream, and, in an instant, he brought me right back to where I'd been with my father. He gave me a shot to knock me out when he was done, and when I tried to tell the Counselor about it the next day, he explained that it was probably just a dream. Like a flashback that seemed very real. In that moment something snapped inside of me, and I could feel the rage building. I managed to maintain my composure long enough to get back to the common area, but the first time that orderly turned his back, I grabbed a chair and hit him with all of my strength. Since it caught him off guard, he fell to the floor, and I wildly slammed him with the chair until several other orderlies pulled me off of him. I know in my heart that had they not come, I would have beaten him to death.

That was the beginning of my transition from being a patient in the hospital to eventually becoming a convict in the penitentiary. Every time I seemed ready to turn a corner something would happen, and this uncontrollable rage would come out of me. It was a vicious cycle, and I didn't know how to get out of it. Though I hoped to one day get out of prison, I just assumed that this anger would always be with me. I was in the midst of serving a three to five year sentence for assault on the day that Billy showed up."

XI. Beginning Again

Listening to Jared's story was emotionally exhausting, and I could tell that it was draining for him, as well. I was grateful to not have any more details about the years between the fire and Jared's reunion with Billy. I interpreted the fact that he'd compressed those years into a couple of sentences to mean that he really didn't want to discuss it either. What he had shared was helpful in understanding the forces that had shaped his life, and he now seemed to want to hand the conversation to Billy. Billy also seemed to sense this, and he picked up the story, right on cue.

"I guess it would be true to say that I never really stopped thinking and praying about Jared. Anytime he'd begin to fade from my memory, I would see him in my dreams or during my prayer times. I would often get excited about trying to find him, but my mother would remind me that if it was truly ordained by God, He would open that door for me. After several years, I learned to just pray for Jared whenever he came to my mind, assuming that I'd never actually see him again. But on my twenty-third birthday I had an incredibly vivid dream of Jared in a cage. The door to the cage was open, but he didn't seem to notice. In the dream I kept trying to get his attention, but couldn't. When I woke up, I prayed for Jared and didn't think much more about it. But the next night I had the same dream again, which had never happened to me before; and after having that same dream for a third night in a row, it was clear to me that God was trying to get my attention.

I knew that the court records from his first trial were sealed, but I couldn't think of any other place to start, so I began looking for anything I could find about the case. I stumbled upon his aunt's name in a newspaper article, and I decided to see if I could find her. Despite the fact that she'd moved and that her last name had changed, God led me to her. I went by the old address, and one of the neighbors knew that she'd remarried, and another remembered the area she was moving to. Though it took several stops, I eventually found her and was able to convince her that I was Jared's friend."

Billy stopped and smiled at Jared, "I guess that last part may not have been exactly true at the time."

Jared smiled back at him knowingly, as Billy continued with the story.

"I'd pre-arranged the visit with the prison, so that I wouldn't catch Jared off guard. I assumed that if he didn't want to see me, he'd let them know. So when I got there and everything was still a 'go,' I figured Jared was OK with the meeting. What I didn't know was that Jared had no idea who they were talking about."

Jared interrupted Billy and added, "They told me that some child psychologist named William Turner wanted to talk to me. I had no idea that they were talking about 'Lil Billy Turner.' Honestly, even after seeing him, I wasn't sure who he was. Once he explained, I recognized him, and after he told me about his dream I figured that he was the same religious nut that he'd been in grade school. But, in a weird way, I was touched that he even remembered me and that he was willing to go through what he did to find me. I didn't know what to do with those feelings, but they kept me from sending him away."

Billy smiled at the recollection and added, "I was at a loss as to what to say to him as well. He clearly didn't trust me, and I didn't really have anything but the dream to go on. We spent a few awkward moments together, and I agreed to leave my information with the prison so that he could get a hold of me if he wanted to. When I left that day, I felt like I had been obedient and that I probably wouldn't ever hear from Jared again."

Jared nodded in agreement and said, "Yeah, I will say that I was confused by the idea that you'd leave your information, because I couldn't conjure a scenario in which I might want to call you. Of course, that was before God gave me some dreams of my own."

I once again tingled with a sense of electricity in the anticipation of hearing how God had intervened in Jared's life. As I glanced over at Katherine, she squeezed my hand and smiled knowingly. So often life just seems to spin out of control and in those times faith can seem like a fairy tale. Thus there seems to be a sense of vindication that accompanies any revelation that God is truly in control. Before Jared could speak of his dreams, the food began to arrive and Billy briefly left us to call and check on MJ. When he returned, we joined hands to bless the food and began looking at each other, wondering who might lead the prayer. In typical Billy fashion, he said, "You are the father at this table, Mr. Davis, so won't you lead us?" Jared nodded in agreement. I was genuinely honored by that, and after we prayed Billy explained that MJ would still be joining us, but that it would be for dessert and coffee afterward. Though I was still mildly curious about this mystery person, I was too excited to hear about Jared's dreams to give it much thought. In between bites Jared continued his story.

"The night that Billy visited I had an incredibly vivid dream, which was unheard of for me. I almost never dreamed, and when I did, they never made any sense. But this dream was very different, and I could tell right away that it meant something. In the dream, I was walking along this long dirt road. It seemed to go on forever, and I was roasting in the sun. As

I shuffled along I was wishing that I didn't have to walk, and I felt like I was never going to get to my destination this way. Just then, Billy tapped me on the shoulder, and handed me a train ticket. But, instead of being thankful, I told him that it didn't do me any good, because there is no train station around. At that, Billy smiled, pointed over my shoulder and said, 'What's that over there?' When I turned around, I found myself standing right in front of a train platform. In the dream I was thinking, 'There's no way I missed seeing that station' and when I turned back around to ask Billy about it, he was gone. That was the end of the dream, and, to be honest, I probably would have forgotten about it except for the fact that I had that exact same dream for the next two nights. I still had no clue as to what to do with it, but it burned in me that something was going on. Even though I couldn't stop thinking about it, I was too stubborn to call Billy."

Jared must have noticed the confused look on my face, because when he saw me, he paused, and I asked, "Why didn't you want to call?"

"Honestly, I'm not really sure. I guess I didn't want to admit that I might need help. But truthfully, I really didn't see how talking to Billy was going to help anyway."

"Had you ever considered what your life might be like after prison?" I asked.

"Not that I can remember. I guess I kind of felt like prison was my destiny. I was born into my father's prison and had spent the rest of my formative years in one institution after another. When I was young, I was sure that I would die before I became an adult. When I reached adulthood I figured that there would always be someone to mess with me and that I'd just keep getting more and more time added to my sentence. I seemed to be in a death spiral, with little hope that things would ever change. I believe that if I'd allowed myself to think about life on the outside it probably would have scared me, because, as bad as prison was, my time in the world had been even worse."

We again sat in silence, as the weight of Jared's words pressed against us. It was Katherine who finally spoke.

"So what finally turned things?" she asked.

Jared gave a shallow smile, as he seemed to be recalling the moment. "Believe it or not, it was my love of reading," he said, as he looked up for our reaction.

"Reading!" I said, in a surprised manner that seemed to please him.

"Yes, since I'd learned that being around people was danger-ous, reading had become a sort of safe haven for me. I really loved crime novels, especially ones that included court room battles. I checked out everything the prison libraries had, and I even had them order me books on occasion. I'm sure that my own experience within the judicial system made the whole process seem very alive to me, and, right before Billy had shown up, the prison librarian had talked to me about some college correspondence courses that I could take for free. I had ordered them and pretty much forgotten about the whole thing, until a couple of week's after Billy's visit. When I first looked at the material I was sure that I wouldn't be able to get through it, but once I got started, it really seemed to click with me, and I began to devour these books. As I'd complete as-signments and tests, the librarian would package that stuff in an envelope and send it off. What I didn't know then was that some of those papers would find their way to Billy."

Katherine and I exchanged another glace, as we once again recognized God's invisible hand reaching into this seemingly hopeless situation. Our attention then shifted to Billy for an explanation of how he'd come to see Jared's work.

Billy's tone reminded me of when he was a little boy, as he explained, "You've got to realize how incredible the odds were against something like this. At that time I was working on my doctorate and was part of a research project on non-tradition-al forms of education. As we got into the research one of the aspects we decided to look at was standardized curriculums, which were administered in non-traditional settings. One of those models was for correctional facilities. A few months af-ter I'd gone to see Jared I was reading through some essays which had been submitted by prisoners as part of their cor-respondence courses, and, wouldn't you know, I came across something with his name on it. I thought I was going to fall out of the chair, and after I read the paper, I knew I had to get back with him."

"Why, what was it that made you so sure?" Katherine asked.

"It was the essay itself. It was about the judicial process and it was fantastic. I couldn't believe how well written it was, and the depth of the insights for a first year college student were amazing. When I looked at the requirements for this particu-lar essay, I realized that he had written about three times more than what they'd required. In that moment I knew that God had given Jared something very special, and I felt certain that he would have no way of understanding just how special it was. For the first time, I could see how I might be able to ac-tually help him."

Jared seemed slightly embarrassed by Billy's assessment of his talent, as his face turned noticeably red. After a quick bite, Billy continued.

"I had all sort sorts of connections with all kinds of educational programs, and I thought if I could get Jared to agree to it, we could probably set up a great program for him to get his degree. I figured that might be a tough sell with him, and I was right. At first he didn't seem to want any part of it."

Confusion must have been written all over our faces as we turned back to Jared because before anyone said anything, he responded, "I know, I know, it was crazy, but I had a hard time believing that I was college material, and I was still trying to figure out what Billy's agenda was. I couldn't really understand why he was so eager to help me. I agreed to keep taking some courses, but I wasn't really willing to commit to a complete 'program', though, I'll admit that I didn't really know what that was. What I didn't realize was that Billy had connected with the prison librarian and that he had essentially become Billy's eyes, ears, and mouthpiece. Every time I mentioned needing something, it seemed to magically appear. Within a couple of months I had a laptop, access to all sorts of incredible software programs, and people who didn't know me from Adam sending me materials that I needed. It was great!"

"So, how did you find out that it was Billy?" I interrupted.

"I was in for my annual meeting with the warden, and I thanked him for all the prison had been doing to help me. That's when he explained that it was Billy who was actually facilitating the whole thing. I tried to be mad about that, but I couldn't really think of why I should be, and so I decided to stop fighting it. For the first time that I could remember I had a goal, and I had a real desire to achieve it, and, if someone wanted to help me, why shouldn't I let them. It was the first time that I had a sense that there might be a future for me, and that I might actually have a life outside of prison. I decided to start meeting with Billy regularly and seeing what he had to say. Once we started doing that, everything really took off."

Billy was visibly excited by this part of the story, as he chimed in, "He was an awesome student, and, because of his confinement, he was able to take more than a full course load. He was well into his third year courses in just a year and a half, and we had to keep resetting the schedule because he was going so fast. He was on a course to finish a four-year Pre-Law degree in just over two years, until unforeseen circumstances changed everything."

Billy's expression and the cryptic way he had ended the sentence made it clear that he wanted Jared to tell this part of the story, and, without missing a beat, he did.

"When all this started, I had three years to go on my sentence, and because of my history of violence, no one considered parole even a remote possibility. But those eighteen months had really changed things. With all my energy focused on learning, I didn't really have the time or the inclination to get into it with anybody. A lot of guys had even tried to bait me into a fight, but I found myself just walking away from them. For the first time I felt as though I had something to lose. I guess the staff must have noticed, because without my requesting it, there was a hearing scheduled to review my sentence and to consider an early release. I almost felt like they were talking about someone else at this hearing, they made me sound like I was some sort of 'model prisoner,' and, as I thought about it, I guess for that period, I was.

Though I now had an incentive to get out, I was also filled with apprehension about whether I could cope in the real world, and whether I'd be able to finish the program we'd started. But, regardless of whether I felt ready, the California Penal system decided I was, and preparations began for my release. I got it into my head that I'd better finish my third year requirements before I got out, and so those last few months in prison were like a blur."

As Jared seemed to ebb, Billy picked the conversation back up. "I remember telling him that there really wasn't any need to rush through that material, but it turned out to be good that he did. The transition out of prison took a lot longer and was a lot rougher than either of us had expected. We knew that he wasn't going to be able to do school while he transitioned through the half-way house, but it turned out to be another year after that before we got back to the 'program' that we'd talked about."

Jared nodded in agreement, and with a decidedly more somber tone he explained, "Yeah, I can say that I almost didn't make it through that period. Getting back out into the world opened a floodgate inside of me, and I felt totally unprepared to cope with it. Fear, anger, perversion… they all seemed to be pulling at me and I found myself looking for a way to escape. I'd be ashamed for people to know the kinds of things that were going on inside of me at that time. It seemed inevitable that I was either going to kill someone or that I'd eventually destroy myself. One night, when I was at the end of my proverbial rope, I was lying in my bed, fantasizing about dying, when my cell-phone rang. It was Billy, and I didn't really want to hear another pep-talk from him, so I didn't answer it.

Somehow he seemed to know how close to the edge I was, because, within a few minutes, he came bursting through the door. He was emotional in a way I'd never seen him before, and he kind of got in my face about not answering his call, so I cursed him and told him to get out. He just looked at me with that weird look he gets and all of a sudden he became eerily calm. In this real low voice he says, 'Have you thought about what comes next?' which, at the time, seemed like a ridiculous question. I spit back some string of expletives about how there was no 'next' – only death. But then he started saying things like I was going to live forever and that leaving this world was just going to propel me into the next one. Even though part of me knew that this was just his religious talk, there was something absolutely compelling in it for me. It suddenly occurred to me that death may not really be a way of escape, but I told him I didn't care, that going to hell didn't scare me. At first, he just gave me a crazy look, and then he said the cruelest thing that anyone has ever said to me."

Both Katherine and I glanced at Billy to check his reaction to Jared's assessment of his words, and from his expression it appeared as though he considered himself guilty as charged. It was hard for me to imagine Billy saying anything that could be considered cruel, but apparently he had. Jared didn't leave us wondering, as he went on to share Billy's words.

"He said to me, 'You realize that your father will be there to welcome you home, don't you?' I was stunned that he'd say something like that, but just like everything else he'd been saying that night, I somehow believed that it was true. I wanted to rage at him, because I had learned to use anger as a way to get through difficult or painful moments, but instead I began to weep uncontrollably. I instantly became sick to my stomach, and I felt as though a bomb had gone off inside of me. In that moment I felt just like I had on that last night with my father; powerless, ravaged, naked, and without hope. The difference was, for the first time in my life, death didn't seem inviting anymore."

We again sat in awkward silence, as Katherine and I absorbed the desperation of the moment Jared was describing, and as he and Billy relived it in their minds. I thought I discerned tears in Billy's eyes, though his face was too downcast to really be sure. While Billy was clearly not proud of what he'd said, I completely understood why he'd said it. I would have said so, but I understood that only Jared could be the one to declare Billy forgiven; and after a few moments, he did.

"Billy saved my life that night; I don't think that there was anything else that could have been said that would have made me change my mind. He was really the only friend I had at that moment, and I'd been putting him through hell for months. It would have been so easy for him to have thrown up his hands and walked away, but he just wouldn't do it. I never really understood why it mattered so much to him, but that night we talked in a way that we never had before. After years of expecting him to preach at me, he finally told me what he believed, and why. He explained that God was the only thing that gave him hope or allowed him to be at peace. As much of a nut as I'd always thought he was, everything he said sounded true to me. After a few years of being around him, I couldn't help but admire who he was and admit that he seemed to have something inside of him that seemed to be missing in me. He didn't push me to make a decision or even to agree with him, but he said that if I was ever going to truly live, I'd have to find something that would give me hope and that would allow me to come to peace with both my past and my future.

He just let those thoughts hang in the air, and because he didn't push me, I didn't push back. I remembered being a little boy, and praying, and maybe even believing, and then I began to wonder when exactly that had changed for me. But as memories of my father came flooding back to the surface, I remembered and I asked Billy, 'If God is real, and He really cares about me, then why didn't He help me when I needed Him most?' Billy just gave me one of those otherworldly looks and said, 'He was there!' Of course, I had no idea what he was talking about, but he told me to close my eyes and to remember the night of the fire. It was hard at first, because I'd learned to block those memories, but he kept pushing and soon I was there.

I could feel the heat, I could smell the stench of everything that had been going on, I could feel my body aching from the abuse, and I could feel the desperate oppression of being a trapped animal. It was as if I'd been completely transported back in time, and then Billy started asking me questions. He asked why I was awake, when everyone else was unconscious, but of course I had no idea why. So, Billy tells me that I need to ask God where He was at that moment, and, after wrestling with that idea for a second, I finally did."

Tears filled Jared's eyes, and he became choked with emotion. He cleared his throat and took a deep breath, before continuing.

"All of a sudden I could see what looked to be some kind of angel, moving past my father's unconscious body and standing over me. It covered my naked body with this blanket, and it began to gently shake my shoulders and whisper in my ear, 'Wake up, Jared, the house is on fire, wake up, Jared, wake up!' When I woke up, he was kneeling right beside me, but in all of the smoke I couldn't see him. When I tried to crawl, I felt like I had no strength, but I saw this angel take hold of the end of the blanket and slowly pull my body down the hall and away from the fire. At the bathroom, I saw him pull me to my feet and turn me to the bathroom window, and he again whispered in my ear. He said, 'The flames are not your home, Jared. Go and don't look back!'"

Again, a wave of emotion came over Jared, and he had to pause, but this time he didn't bother to regain his composure. Through his tears and with broken words, he said, "And suddenly I knew that Billy was right, that God had been there in the burning house that night, and that it was He who made sure I got out. And something about the words He'd said changed everything for me. He said that the flames were not my home, which told me that I wasn't destined to become my father or to follow in his footsteps. And when he said not to look back, I sensed that I'd somehow been released from that past, and that there was something better waiting down the road for me. I felt as though a boulder had been lifted off my chest, and as if I were taking my very first breaths.

Billy and I talked into the wee hours of the morning, and, by the time we were done, I knew that I was finally free, and that I had a Father who really loved me!"

By now we were all an emotional mess, and no one seemed interested in finishing their food. Just as I had marveled at the revelation that little Billy had grown into Dr. Billy, so it was with Jared Lowe, whose story was somehow even more unlikely than Billy's had been. Katherine excitedly told Jared and Billy about the dream she'd had earlier that afternoon, in which she'd encountered the grown Jared, walking away from the burning house and seemingly unwilling to look back. She'd been right when she'd concluded that the dream wasn't about Jared's lack of concern for his parents. I could now see that the dream was about Jared walking away from his past.

The emotional roller-coaster of the whole day was beginning to take its toll on me, and so I ordered some coffee from our bewildered waiter, who by now seemed genuinely afraid to approach the table. I had no doubt that we'd been quite a spectacle, but I couldn't seem to muster any real concern over what other people might be thinking. This evening had been far too rich for regrets. Jared and Billy both went on to share bits and pieces about the changes that had taken place in Jared's life. We learned that he had gone on to finish his final year of college, that he'd graduated with distinction and that he was now working as a legal aid for a prestigious law firm. As Jared finished that part of the story he said, "And that's where MJ comes in."

That caught me somewhat off guard, because I'd assumed that MJ was Billy's associate. When I asked about it, Billy started to explain, "MJ is Jared's boss," but before he got a chance to say anymore, Jared interrupted by saying, "Speak of the devil." Immediately both Billy and Jared jumped to their feet, as a stunningly beautiful blonde woman approached us. As she reached the table, she turned and smiled at Katherine and me, as Billy said, "Mr. and Mrs. Davis, this is my fiancé,

MJ." I stumbled to my feet, wondering if I'd heard Billy right, when MJ extended her hand toward us and said, "That's actually Michelle Johnson, and it's a great pleasure to meet you both." Her handshake was surprisingly firm, yet, at the same time, very warm. Billy pecked her lightly on the cheek as he pulled out her chair, and she clearly reveled in his attention. As she sat, Jared said, "Hey, boss," to which she playfully responded, "Good evening, Mr. Lowe." And as I watched these three attractive young people smile at each other I realized that this evening was far from over.

XII. Daddy's Girl

MJ's arrival seemed to change the atmosphere at the table and to shift the focus from the past to the present tense. As much as I had been the one to initiate that retrospective, I was relieved at the lighter tone of the conversation. MJ apologized profusely for missing dinner and quickly ordered a salad. I caught myself watching her as she interacted with Billy, Jared, the waiter, and Katherine. I was impressed by her demeanor, which was at once direct, and, yet, not at all domineering. Despite her statuesque beauty and the fact that she was apparently an influential lawyer, she seemed surprisingly down-to-earth. It occurred to me that she was, in many ways, like Billy's mother, Susan. That thought made me smile and gave me the sense that Billy had undoubtedly found his soul-mate. Like so many other things that had happened in the last few days, it seemed as though God's own hand was somehow moving things into place. Though I still didn't have any clue as to what to expect, it felt good to be a part of it.

Katherine quizzed MJ on how she and Billy had met, and it was not at all surprising to learn that it had been through Jared, who light-heartedly teased at how long it took them to finally consent to a date. Billy blushed, as he weakly claimed that it was their dedication to their careers that had slowed the process, but even he didn't seem to believe that. MJ gave a shallow shrug, offering no excuse. After some more gentle ribbing from Jared, Billy decided to come clean.

"The truth is that I judged the book by its cover," he said pensively. "I saw this beautiful, successful lawyer, and I really wasn't interested. I figured that we'd have nothing in common, and I really didn't want to get involved in her world. Jared kept telling me that she wasn't who I thought she was, but I found myself evading his attempts to set us up."

MJ smiled at Billy's admission and added, "As bad as that may sound, I did the same thing to him. Jared went on about what a great guy Billy was, but I couldn't seem to get past my own ideas about what a 'college professor' might be like. Since I wasn't really looking for a relationship, avoiding the whole dating scene seemed like the best tact."

"So, what finally broke the ice with you two?" I asked.

Billy smiled and said, "Jared was part of the Christmas pageant at his church, and he invited us to come watch. Of course, he didn't let either of us know that he'd invited the other, and then we had to sit at the same table while he went and did his thing in the program. Though we didn't get much of a chance to talk, it was enough for us to get past some of our misconceptions."

"Yup!" Jared broke in, "I was apparently typecast as a 'Wise Man' in that pageant!"

We all laughed, and then Katherine asked Billy, "So what was it about Michelle that was so different than what you expected?"

Billy flashed a sheepish smile toward MJ before addressing Katherine. "I guess I expected someone in her position to be very goal oriented, which isn't necessarily a bad thing, unless it causes you to be callous about people's feelings. I've often noticed that overachievers can be somewhat ruthless when it comes to their fellow man, and I guess I had my guard up for that. I was also probably a little prejudiced toward lawyers in general, as I tend to be more into the spirit of law than the letter of the law. But that night at Jared's church I watched her interact with people and noticed how she smiled warmly and didn't seem to condescend to anyone. I saw her eat chicken and noodles off a paper plate and sincerely compliment the older church ladies on how good it was, and I even caught her playing peek-a-boo with a toddler at the next table over. As if all of that wasn't enough, I saw the tears in her eyes when the actor in the Christmas pageant presented the Christ child, and I finally realized that Jared was right. I had totally misjudged her."

At that point Jared interrupted, "What was that you said?"

"You mean, the part about misjudging her?" Billy asked wryly.

"No, no, before that; the part about Jared being right. That's my favorite part," he said, as we all laughed.

Jared then smiled at MJ and said, "Go ahead, now you tell your side of the story, you know that part about how I was right about Billy, too!"

With a look of mock indignation, MJ said, "My, Mr. Lowe, we are a bit starved for affirmation tonight, aren't we?"

After a few chuckles, Katherine said to MJ, "I would like to hear your take on that evening as well."

MJ smiled weakly and said, "I guess my story is pretty much the same as Billy's. I expected a somewhat pretentious, intellectual guy, who would be pretty impressed with himself, and, instead, I found this warm, caring person. When I came into the lobby that night I saw him helping some little boy with his shepherd costume. Then in line for food, I heard him have a five minute conversation with this older lady about how she kept the lumps out of her mashed potatoes. I was amazed that he appeared to be truly interested in what she had to say.

And as I watched the scene with the Christ child that night, I could see the tears in his eyes, too." MJ's voice cracked a little at the end, as she seemed to be emotional at the memory. After taking a moment to regain her composure a devious grin broke across her face, and, in a mellow-dramatic voice, she said, "And that's when I realized that Jared was right. Oh, how could I ever have doubted him! After all, he'd never been wrong about anything else before!"

Again, we drank in the medicine of a good laugh, and just as the moment was about to pass, Jared rolled his eyes and added the barb, "I could have told you that he was no intellectual."

As a fresh wave of laughter hit, we all turned to Billy, waiting for his comeback. Blinking at us innocently, he said, "What, I really did want to know how to keep the lumps out of my mashed potatoes."

I couldn't tell if that was as funny as it seemed, or if we were just getting slap-happy, but I laughed like I hadn't laughed in a long time.

Our waiter warily approached the table with MJ's salad, and he seemed genuinely relieved to see that our tears had somehow turned to laughter. Though I wanted to hear more of MJ's story, I tried to be considerate of the fact that she was now trying to eat her dinner. Billy moved the conversation in a different direction when he said to Jared, "I'm sure the Davis' would love to hear about your better half as well." Jared blushed, as his quick witted banter dissolved into shy, schoolboy embarrassment. He tried to say that no one wanted to hear about that, but Katherine absolutely insisted.

With some reluctance he shared the story of how he'd met a young woman at church, who'd grown up in an abusive home and who'd been in an abusive marriage that ended when her former husband was sent to prison for assault and domestic violence. He explained that both of them had pretty much come to the conclusion that they were incapable of having a healthy relationship, and that both were trying to accept the fact that they were meant to be alone. He said that though they'd initially committed to the idea of being nothing more than friends, their friendship had grown into a genuine love that took them both by surprise. He confessed that though they believed that God had brought them together, they were still moving very cautiously toward marriage.

In the time it had taken Jared to tell us about his fiancé MJ had finished her salad, and she added, "You should see them together; they're really a beautiful couple. I marvel at how God uses even the most hurtful things from our past as a way to move us toward some more hopeful end."

Jared nodded in agreement, "It's true, I don't know anyone who could really understand some of my struggles other than someone who's experienced these things first hand. Even though we've both come to this relationship with all sorts of emotional baggage, God somehow uses our hurtful pasts as a conduit for healing. Though we still have some anxiety, we've really come a long way, and I believe that God will take us the rest of the way."

Katherine seemed very moved by Jared's story, and I could tell that her mothering instinct was stirred for him, as she asked, "What is it that you fear, Jared?"

He bowed his head and in a low voice he said, "That I'm going to wake up one morning after we're married and find out that I'm really my father, and that I'll somehow hurt her like every other man who ever said he loved her."

Tears streamed down Katherine's face, and her voice became almost stern as she reached across the table in front of me and grasped Jared's hands. As his eyes rose to meet hers she said, "You are not your father, and you are not like your father, and you will never be like your father. Before you were in your mother's womb the God of Heaven knew you, and it was He who knit you together within her. He did not create you in their image, He created you in His own image. All of your days were written in His book before one of them came to pass, and all of the hairs on your head have been numbered by Him.

There is no force in heaven or on earth, save your own free will, that could ever propel you down the path your father chose to travel. God has not left you an orphan. In fact, He has placed the very power of heaven within you. When you are weak, He is strong and He will never leave you nor forsake you. He has not given you a spirit of fear; He has given you a sound mind, and you must take every thought captive. Be ruthless with every high and lofty thought that exalts itself against the knowledge of who He is and of who He made you to be. He has set you free from the things of the past, the old man has passed away, and, behold, all things have been made new."

I knew that Katherine could have gone on, but I think she became aware of all the eyes that were staring at her, so she stopped. Jared's tearful eyes let her know that he'd heard her, as he quietly whispered, "Thank you." MJ touched Katherine's shoulder and then pulled her into an embrace. "That was beautiful; it reminded me of my father. He could speak out the scriptures with such authority, and to my ears, it was like poetry. I remember being a little girl and watching him preach. He had such passion, and the people just seemed to hang on his every word. You have that same passion and that same wonderful gift."

As the ladies once again embraced, I thought of how amazing it was that we had all become so deeply connected in such a short time. This whole evening had such an other-worldly feel to it and, despite a gnawing sense of fatigue, I found myself not wanting the night to end. MJ's remembrance of her father only piqued my curiosity about her story, and so, after we ordered dessert and coffee, I asked her about it.

"My parents were lifelong missionaries, and I was their only child. Early on, the doctors told my mother that she was incapable of having children, which my parents saw as a confirmation of their calling to the mission field. They served in Central and South America for years, and one day, a tribal woman came to them and told my mother that she would have a child in her fortieth year. My parents immediately dismissed what she'd said, and they'd long since forgotten about it, when I was conceived and born in my mom's fortieth year.

For the most part, I grew up living in grass huts, with dirt floors and amongst the indigenous people of whatever region we were assigned to. At his heart my father was a teacher, and normally he'd start a school for the children wherever we would go. Though my mother taught me at home, I'd often attend his classes with the native children, and I was mesmerized by his teaching. Many times we were in very hostile situations, but my father always seemed in command of himself and the people around him. When I was thirteen we were living in a region that was being controlled by the local drug lords, and my father wanted to send my mother and me back to the United States. But, my mother put her foot down and insisted that if God could protect him, He could protect us, as well. Eventually, these criminals came to view my father as some sort of threat, and they began a campaign of intimidation, hoping that we would leave. There were several small incidents at first, and when that didn't work, they burned the school to the ground. But dad was convinced that God had sent us to this place, and so, he kept on teaching the children and preaching to the people of the village.

A few weeks after the school was destroyed a group of men came in the night with guns and took my father. My mother and I were terrified that we'd never see him again, and for the next several months we tried to work with the missionary organization, the local authorities, and even the US embassy to locate him. No one seemed to know anything, and we began to fear the worst. After almost a year we returned to the United States, believing that my father must be dead. Not long after we got back my mother got a call from the US Consulate, saying that they'd received word that my father was in prison, and that he had been charged with some kind of sedition against the government.

It was all very confusing, but we returned immediately and were able to see him. He had clearly been beaten, and he'd lost a lot of weight, but his spirit was still strong. With help from the embassy a legal team was formed to help my dad, but it still took almost another year before he came to trial. Once the trial began it was clear that the government had no case, and soon after that, they agreed to release my father if he'd agree to leave the country. Just after my sixteenth birthday we returned home with my dad. Sadly, his years of incarceration had left him sickly and broken down, and just before my eighteenth birthday he passed away from heart and respiratory failure."

Tears crept from the sides of MJ's eyes, as she paused to dab them. "His life was such a testimony to me, and watching the way the legal system was manipulated played a big part in my decision to become a lawyer. There is rarely a day that goes by that I don't think of something my father said or did, and I feel as though his faith is still a source of strength for me. Even though my mom is in her seventies she still works with the missionary organization, helping to prepare people who are heading out to the field. She is an amazing woman, and I feel really blessed to still have her."

Billy added, "Yes, Mrs. Davis, I think you and Mrs. Johnson would make a great team."

Katherine beamed at him and softly said, "Now, Billy, you promised to call me Katherine."

Billy blushed and nodded in agreement before continuing on. "I truly believe that God orchestrated this evening, and that He's brought us together tonight for more than just an opportunity to catch up on the years we've missed. I feel like the story MJ just shared relates to the legal case that she's been involved with for the last couple of years. It has to do with the education system and people within the government wanting to take away a parent's right to choose how their children are taught. Just as the local drug lords viewed her father's teaching of the children as a threat to them, there are those in this country who view home school and other forms of non-traditional education as some sort of danger to society. Not long ago I was drawn into the work that she and Jared are doing, and now I sense that you guys are being pulled in as well."

For the life of me, I couldn't imagine how we might be involved in the case Billy described, and I could tell by the look on Katherine's face that she didn't see it either. But, that strange tingling sensation that I'd gotten so many times in the last couple of days seemed to indicate that invisible forces were indeed at work, so I resisted my urge to counter what Billy had suggested and decided to hear him out.

XIII. The Calling

MJ explained, "Attempts to limit or completely eliminate alternative forms of education are not really new, but this particular effort has some especially troubling aspects. It is very well organized and well funded, and it brings a new slant to the legal argument. These activists chose to file their test case here in Arizona, in hopes that it will set the stage for their real target, which is California. Essentially, they're saying that the state has a duty to educate the children, and that it cannot meet that obligation unless children are taught in state run schools."

"Certainly a parents' right to educate their children as they see fit has been clearly established in the courts by now," I interjected.

"There is a lot of precedence in that direction, but this argument is built around the obligations of the government. On the surface it doesn't sound like much, but it is based on a tactic that has been very successful in Europe, where home school has been outlawed in many countries. They have the backing of the NEA (National Education Association), the NTA (National Teachers Association), and even the United Nations, who is promoting an initiative on children's rights. Essentially, it says that governments should regulate and oversee parents' upbringing of their children. Their primary means of establishing this proposed regulation would be through state-run school systems. When we first took this case on we figured it would be pretty straight forward, but many of our state officials have bowed to the political pressure, and the battle has been far more fierce than we expected. There have even been points where I thought we might lose this thing."

Billy added, "This is why you saw me on television, Mr. Davis, I was testifying before congressional hearings on the validity of non-traditional forms of education. If you'd have tuned in sooner you would have probably seen our old friend, Mike Skinner, as well."

"You're kidding me. Did you guys come face to face?" I asked.

"Yes, but I'm pretty sure he didn't make the connection at first. He was very cordial before the proceedings, but when it came out that I had been expelled from the public school system he looked as though he'd seen a ghost. I really thought he was going to fall out of his chair. Afterwards, he left the room quickly and didn't say a word to anyone," Billy replied.

"I thought he'd retired years ago," I added.

"That's the official story, but he's had his hands in this case from the onset," Billy said.

As I pondered the involvement of Mike Skinner, Katherine voiced what I'd been thinking. "I guess I don't see how Bob and I fit into all of this."

MJ answered, "You guys both have years of experience within the state-run education system, and the one thing that we've really lacked is people with your kind of background who are willing to openly contradict the NEA's or the NTA's position. Though we've been able to find 'experts' on education who are willing to testify, it would really help the credibility of our arguments if people with first-hand knowledge could corroborate them."

"I promise you that I mean no offense with this question, but how can you be sure that we'll agree with your position?" I asked

Billy answered, "Well for me, it is as simple as the fact that I believe we've taken the position that a reasonable person would take, coupled with my belief that you are reasonable people. But probably even more importantly, I have a strong sense that this is why God brought us together here tonight, and, if that's true, I'm sure we'll find plenty of agreement. I don't know how you have perceived the events of the last couple of days, but I've felt as though there has been something almost supernatural going on. I can't remember a time when I've so directly sensed divine intervention. But, even with all of that, it's really up to the both of you. I don't want to pressure you into anything. If this is really what I think it is, then that confirmation needs to come from within, and not from me."

Of course, I couldn't deny the supernatural sense that had accompanied the last few days, and this meeting did seem to be about something more than just old acquaintances getting together. But my mind also reeled at the thought of battling Mike Skinner, the NEA, the NTA, and maybe even the United Nations. I never liked this kind of confrontation, and, at this point in my life, it was the last thing I wanted to be involved with. Oddly, it stirred many of the same emotions that I'd felt twenty-five years earlier as I watched Mike railroad Billy out of the school system. Those feelings once again seemed to convict me of being a coward. It was disappointing to consider that maybe I'd grown so little over the years. Knowing that everyone was waiting for me to respond, I decided to stall.

"So, what are the chances that you will be successful with this case?" I asked.

MJ beat Billy to the punch, saying, "We've already been successful at the state level, but now the case is being appealed into the federal court system, where they ultimately hope to make their arguments to the Supreme Court. This is where it could get interesting, as the judicial activism in the federal courts is far more pervasive, and the political influence of the NEA could be more profound. Though it is a positive sign that we've done well in these lower courts, we can't assume that it will be the same fight at the next level. The stakes are definitely getting higher, and we need to try to cover all of our bases, but, with that said, I agree with Billy in that we're not here to talk you into this. In my life I've found that the only reason to engage in a battle like this is because you feel called to it, so, unless you're feeling that calling I don't know that I would go forward with it."

"I absolutely agree with that," Billy said. "You need to be sure that this is your fight."

"Do you think that this has impacted your standing at the university?" I asked Billy.

"To some degree, I'm sure that it has. I've been encouraged in subtle ways to distance myself from the case, but nothing has officially been said. I'm really not crossing any sort of ethical boundary with my involvement, so I doubt that any formal action could be taken, but certain people's perception of me could be affected, which may result in consequences down the road. The thing is, I do feel called to this battle and not just because MJ is leading the legal team. As I look back on what happened to me and at how God raised me up from there, I can't help but feel that it was for such a time as this. I don't know what this battle will cost me, and God certainly isn't going to guarantee the outcome, but there is no better place to be than where He's called you to be."

Billy's words pierced me, as I could see a faith in him that I found lacking in myself. In principle, I agreed with his assertion about being where God called you to be, but I found myself not wanting to hear that calling. I loved the quiet life that

Katherine and I had settled into. I liked working in the yard with her and taking leisurely walks. I'd really looked forward to this season of life, and I wasn't in a hurry to trade it in for the strife of a battle that could possibly go on for years. I guess on some level I had viewed our retirement years as a reward for a race well run, and so, the idea that the race may not be over wasn't exactly welcome news. But as I considered our beautiful home and our manicured lawn through the lens of eternity, I had to admit that it looked a lot like a monument that we'd built to ourselves or maybe even to the "American Dream."

Even so, I found myself wanting to fight the idea that we were somehow meant to be involved with all of this. I could see how Billy's experience made him the perfect person for his role in the case, and I could see that for MJ as well, but couldn't any old retired teachers fill the role they were asking us to play? There was a part of me that yearned to put on the helmet and charge out onto the battlefield, and yet, there was another part of me that wanted to curl up in a ball and hide under the covers. Were all those hair-raising, tingling sensations of the last twenty-four hours God's way of tapping me on the shoulder, or was it just my excitement at seeing Billy and Jared again? I could see the questioning look in their eyes, but I felt paralyzed at the thought of giving a definitive answer. Jared broke the tension of the moment by speaking up.

"One of my favorite scriptures is the one that says that, 'God works all things to the good, for those who love Him and who are called to His purposes,' and I feel like that would apply to each of us. Of course, we all know my story and Billy's story, but then there is MJ losing her father the way she did, and Mrs. Davis being widowed with young children, and there was your first marriage, Mr. Davis. Each of us has had difficult and painful things happen to us, and yet, wouldn't we all say that God has somehow worked these things to our good? It hasn't been easy, and often it is difficult to see what is being accomplished, but, in hindsight, it is always clear that He was working. What are the odds that we would find each other after all these years, and what are the odds that all these pieces would fit together so perfectly? If we focus on the future there are all sorts of question marks, but, as I look around this table tonight, it is impossible to deny God's ability to work in and through the lives of His people. The question isn't, 'What does the future hold?' or, 'Will we win this case?' or even, 'How do I feel about all of this?' The question is, 'Where are we called to be?' And, 'What is our role?' In the end, that is all a servant can hope to do for his master."

Jared had absolutely boiled it down to a place that I could no longer wrestle with the facts. He was right, if I claimed to be a follower, the only question that needed to be answered was, "Where am I supposed to be?" As I looked to Katherine I could see that she had something to say, and so I asked, "What is it?"

Katherine then shared the dream she'd had that afternoon, where she saw us sitting at the defense table in a courtroom. I couldn't believe that I'd already forgotten about that, and as she described the picture it finally seemed undeniable to me that we were, in fact, being drawn into this. It was also clear to me that Katherine had come to that conclusion long before I had. As much as I'd wrestled with the idea there was something truly exhilarating about understanding that we were where we were supposed to be, at the time we were supposed to be there, and that God had something for us to accomplish. As that revelation settled in on me it felt as though anything were possible.

In my mind, I'd made this trip about Billy, but now, I could see that God had really done all this to move Katherine and me into position. He wasn't looking back, He was moving forward. As I looked around the table I felt incredibly fortunate to be a part of something bigger than myself, and, as I took hold of Katherine's hand, I felt overwhelmed with love for these people. Suddenly, I wasn't worried about what might lie ahead, and I realized that little Billy Turner was right. "There is no better place to be than where God's called you to be."

Author's Note:

So whatever happened to "And they all lived happily ever after?" I guess I just can't bring myself to do that because it's not real. I hope that's not a disappointment, but it's a risk I'll have to take. Life and people and relationships are never completely resolved; and no one event, regardless of how positive it may be, alleviates the struggles of tomorrow. If that is true, then the pinnacle of life is likely found in those moments when we are at peace with ourselves, accompanied by people we genuinely care about, filled with a sense of purpose for the present and hopeful about what lies ahead. I would submit that such moments are truly rare and that only a select few ever really experience them. Indeed, most of us go through life with the sense that we never quite fit in, searching for some meaning in the journey and often feeling as though we've arrived a day late and a dollar short. The moment I'm trying to describe is essentially the antithesis of that.

There are some who might wonder about the outcome of the court case, or whether Billy and MJ have children, or whether Jared overcomes his fear of marriage… but ultimately, that misses the point. I think that our need to determine some kind of final score is tied to our obsession with winning. After all, unless we get a final score, we don't know who won. But if it is winning that qualifies us as a "winner", then it is undoubtedly responding to an upward call that qualifies us as a "follower." And in God's economy, I believe that is of far greater worth.

As this story ends the people sitting around that table are experiencing one of those amazing moments, which, to my way of thinking, is as close to "And they all lived happily ever after" as we can get on this side of heaven.

Bryan Corbin

The Ballad of Billy Turner

Bryan Corbin

www.ingramcontent.com/pod-product-compliance
Lightning Source LLC
Chambersburg PA
CBHW021111130626
46554CB00002B/630